THE MAGIC TOUCH

Ann Redmayne

CHIVERS

British Library Cataloguing in Publication Data available

This Large Print edition published by BBC Audiobooks Ltd, Bath, 2008.
Published by arrangement with the Author.

U.K. Hardcover ISBN 978 1 405 64534 8
U.K. Softcover ISBN 978 1 405 64535 5

Printed and bound in Great Britain by
Antony Rowe Ltd., Chippenham, Wiltshire

CHAPTER ONE

It was the loud blast of a car horn which made Fenella Foulds turn away from gazing in delight at the small, sunlit bay many metres below her. 'Can't you see you're blocking the drive?' The girl driving a banana-yellow sports car impatiently pushed designer sunglasses up into her magenta coloured hair. The April sunshine wasn't all that strong, but the sunglasses seemed to go with the girl's bright hair and car.

'Sorry,' Ella flustered, conscious of the fact that she and the girl had nothing in common in either looks or cars.

'If you move your car back a bit,' the driver waved her hand towards a wide gate. 'You can open that for me, then shut it after I've driven through.'

Although feeling she was being treated like a gatekeeper, Ella knew she had been inconsiderate blocking the entrance. Opening the ornamental metal gate, she saw at the end of a short stony drive, a long, low cottage nearly on the edge of the cliff.

How wonderful to have such stunning sea views all the time!

The banana-yellow car swept past her, stopping in front of a small wooden building connected to the cottage by a short path shaded by arches of climbing plants just breaking into leaf. Shutting the gate, Ella craned her neck to see more, just as the girl turned to briefly wave her thanks. Embarrassed at being caught prying, Ella hurriedly turned away.

She drove cautiously down the narrow, steep, zig-zagging road, and by the time she reached the shore her hands were clammy with perspiration. A patch of winter-browned turf by the side of Watch Cottage was the only suitable place to park, but seeing no other vehicle, she frowned as she checked her watch. She was early, but had Audrey Hopkins already left?

Getting out of the car, Ella walked slowly towards Watch Cottage. Slate-roofed, it crouched on higher ground, in front of a small quarry which had provided its stone. But a remarkable feature was a two-storey tower built on the end nearest to her. The top floor's large windows faced the sea and Ella wondered if it had been a lookout, hence its name.

Going towards the door at the opposite end to the tower, Ella was unaware she was being watched by Audrey. A retired, widowed teacher, she had been persuaded by her sister to visit her in Australia for six months. But until she actually saw Ella, she had been reluctant to go, even though travel arrangements had been made.

2

Moving away from the window, Audrey muttered to herself. 'You'll do. I know you'll look after my cottage and exercise Will's dog.'

Although she had been impressed by Ella's letter and references and liked her photograph, seeing her purposeful walk, black hair cut in an easily manageable style, she guessed the girl she was leaving in charge of her much loved cottage would be able to deal with any emergencies. She didn't look the sort to be sent into a tizz by spring gales and high tides.

Just as Ella raised the dolphin-shaped knocker, Audrey opened the door, two big holdalls and capacious handbag obviously ready for her departure.

As she extended a capable hand and introduced herself, Ella asked anxiously, 'Are you going soon?' She had expected to have at least a couple of hours to familiarise herself with Watch Cottage before being left alone.

'No need to hang about. I'll show you the notes I've made of things like shops and doctor.'

All the windows on the ground floor were small to minimise the effect of the storms and winds. The walls were thick, white-painted inside, as well as out.

It didn't take long for Audrey to open cupboards and drawers, then show Ella the instructions for the old, but reliable electric cooker and other equipment.

3

'As you can see, Watch Cottage is small and easy to run,' Audrey said. 'The living room is through there, and beyond used to be a bedroom, but I've made it into a decent bathroom.

'The door in the corner of the bathroom hides the stairs up to the only bedroom which is in the tower. But you can explore after I've gone. I don't feel the cold and I hope you're not a chilly person. The only heating is the open fire in the living room. I've got in a supply of logs and there's a pile of driftwood drying in the lean-to at the back.

'It's surprising how much the tide brings in. Which reminds me, it also brings in plastic bottles, all sorts of things washed overboard or thrown by thoughtless people. I gather them up . . .'

'I really will look after Watch Cottage,' Ella promised softly.

'I know you will. Call me silly, but this small bay, the cottage, they've become so much a part of my life. But enough of that. You don't want to hear my ramblings. Let's go outside. I do wish that taxi would hurry up.' Audrey fretted as they stood looking up at the twisting road. 'Knowing you had a car, I've left mine with Sal at Peace Farm. Perhaps it would have been better if I hadn't. I could have been away by now.'

'Your nearest neighbour must be that cottage perched up there on the ledge,' Ella

4

said, trying to distract her.

'Yes. That had such a pretty name, but when the previous owner, an artist, lived there he called it *The Studio* and although I've hinted he should change it back, Will Kennedy hasn't. It's so important to keep something of the old, don't you think?'

And seeing Ella nod, Audrey continued, 'Modern, new, doesn't necessarily mean excellence. But to get back to Will, since he fell off a ladder and broke his arm, I've been exercising his dog. I know a broken arm doesn't stop him walking Oliver, but he's so busy . . . Will that is, not Oliver!

'It would be a great kindness to them both if you could continue to do the same. It's all written down. But give it a miss at weekends, Linzi's there. She drives a bright yellow car and spells her name L-I-N-Z-I, so you can guess what type of girl she is, all froth, dreadful red hair . . .'

'Why is this called Watch Cottage?' Ella asked hurriedly, for although she guessed she had already met Linzi, albeit briefly, she liked to judge people for herself.

Willingly, Audrey launched into its history. Built about 1850, it had been the home of a fisherman and his family, but when he had been lost in a storm, his wife refused to accept it. Grief stricken, she huddled on the shingle separating the grass from the sand, ignoring the needs of her children. So other fishermen built on the little tower so she could keep watch without catching pneumonia.

'That's really sad,' Ella said, shading her eyes to look up at it.

'You haven't asked if it's haunted. Most young girls would have.'

'No need. It's very peaceful and anyway lots of others will have lived here since then, including you, and as you're reluctant to leave I guess you're very happy here.'

*   *   *

Ella watched the taxi make the slow climb until it was out of sight, and guessing Audrey would be looking back for as long as possible, she waved vigorously. But it wasn't only Audrey who was biting back tears.

Ella too was swamped by emotion. Made redundant when the company she worked for was taken over by a large one, another job was difficult to find in Worcester. Her flatmates who worked elsewhere said she wasn't to worry about her share of rent and expenses, but Ella continued to pay her way, her anxiety mounting as her modest savings shrank.

She had been in the dentist's waiting room thumbing through a country magazine when she saw the advert for a *cottage sitter.* Although the magazine was three months old, on the spur of the moment, she applied, but not very hopefully for the advert asked for a *mature*

6

lady. Was twenty-two mature enough? she wondered as she posted her application.

Her interview with Audrey had been by phone, and here she was with such a complete change of lifestyle that she almost had to pinch herself to make sure it was all really happening.

Unloading her things from the car, she felt reluctant to really look around Watch Cottage, it seemed too much like prying. So first she took her clothes up to the bedroom. The stairs were steep, narrow, and it seemed odd to go into the room without going through a door. At first glance the white walls seemed cold, but as Ella unpacked she began to appreciate the blue and yellow patterned duvet set and curtains which echoed the sea, sky and sand.

Like the rest of the cottage, the furniture was old, but not shabby and Ella guessed Audrey had taken her time furnishing the cottage. It was in an odd way an act of love, but making a home was like that.

Love . . . With a sigh, Ella sank down on to the bed. Would she ever find a man whom she truly loved? She'd had boyfriends all of whom had enjoyed her company, dancing, going out for meals, the cinema, walking. But it was she who always finished with them, much to their surprise and although some asked why, she just shook her head and smiled ruefully. If she said the real reason, that she yearned for a deep relationship, they would have been off like a shot anyway!

It wasn't so much she wanted to marry, just that she wanted to be important to someone, to matter, to share. Share what, she wasn't sure. An only child, both her parents were too busy with their small business to give her much attention, to listen, to talk . . .

Although she had been happy working in the accounts office, Ella had never felt totally satisfied. When she had tried to talk to her flatmates about this, they laughed, telling her the reason they worked was for the money, nothing else.

So although losing her job had been a shock, she had seen it as an opportunity to change the course of her life. Hopefully after six months looking after Watch Cottage, she would know what she really wanted to do.

Audrey had left enough food for a couple of days and so Ella was making her evening meal when a furious scratching and barking at the door made her jump, for all she had heard until then was the cry of seagulls, the rush of the incoming tide. Hurrying to open the door, she was nearly knocked over by the large dog trying to get in. But seeing her, not Audrey, he backed away, tail down, eyes suspicious.

'It's all right,' Ella said softly, crouching down and extending her hand. 'Were you expecting Audrey?' She smiled as the dog put his head on one side at the sound of the name.

Although he came towards her slowly, he

was obviously alert for any sign of Audrey, and remembering her note about Will Kennedy's dog, Ella realised this shaggy-coated, black and white animal must be his. Audrey described Oliver's ancestors as totally without morals, the result being an odd, but attractive mixture of sheepdog, retriever and poodle.

Standing up, she looked down at Oliver who was now wagging his tail. 'Have you come for your walk?' she asked, although Audrey had made it sound as though she collected him every day, mentioning there were steep rough steps cut into the hillside which were good exercise for heart and lungs.

'Or have you escaped? In which case the sooner I get you home the better.'

Going on to the narrow strip of turf which linked cottage with cliff, she called Oliver to follow which he did, frolicking around her, barking. But suddenly glad of company, she stopped, reluctant to return him. Surely a few more minutes wouldn't matter?

Oliver settled the question by dashing down into the sea, barking at seagulls high above him. When Ella laughed this excited him into even wilder antics, chasing his tail, trying to catch strands of floating seaweed.

But even above this noise, he heard the car before she did. Running out of the sea, he sat down beside her, leaning against her legs. Looking down at him, Ella frowned. It was almost as though he was hiding.

9

Then hearing the roar of a powerful engine, Ella guessed it was the banana-yellow car coming down the road.

'You naughty dog, come here at once!' The wind caught the girl's long magenta hair as she leaned out of the window.

But as Oliver pressed himself even closer to Ella, she put a reassuring hand on his head. 'Are you his owner?' she asked.

'No, but what's it to you?' Getting sinuously out of the car, the girl came towards them cautiously, her high heels definitely not suited to walking on yielding, sandy ground.

'Audrey Hopkins has been exercising him, and whilst she's away I'm doing it.'

'Oh, sorry! When I saw you earlier I thought you were just a visitor. I'm Linzi. But I expect Audrey has told you all about me. Although it's nothing to do with her, she'd made it plain that she disapproves of my car, my hair colour. Is your hair naturally that black?' she asked, peering at Ella. 'Yes, I guess it is. I come down at weekends to work for Will. Unfortunately his dog took it into his head to escape and as Will is busy, I said I'd look for the silly nuisance.'

As she spoke, Linzi moved closer to Oliver, but he ran off barking loudly. 'I knew he'd do that,' she sighed, glancing at her watch. 'And I'm already late.'

'If it would help, I'll take him home,' Ella offered. 'When he tires, he'll come back.'

10

Looking at her watch again, Linzi hesitated then 'Thanks! Oliver lives up there,' she said, pointing to the cottage. 'There's no need to disturb Will. Just open the gate for Oliver to go into the garden. I guess you can continue to take him for walks. He's usually in the garden so just take him. Don't disturb Will. Audrey insisted on calling in when she collected Oliver, and again when she brought him back.

'And you'd better move that car of yours. I'm surprised Audrey didn't tell you it was hallowed ground, sacred to dear Joel.'

'Who's Joel?'

'You'll find out soon enough!' was Linzi's enigmatic reply as getting into her car, she roared away.

CHAPTER TWO

When the phone rang in Watch Cottage it was such an intrusive sound that Ella ran to answer it. It would be Audrey checking everything was all right. But it was a man asking brusquely, 'Audrey, have you got Oliver? He's missing.'

'Audrey's not here, and yes, I'm sorry, I have got Oliver.'

'Sorry, I'd forgotten Audrey's gone.'

'I'll bring Oliver back at once.'

'Just see him through the gate.'

As Ella lay in bed that first night, curtains wide open allowing the white light from a full moon to flood the room, she wondered exactly what she had let herself in for. Oliver's owner certainly seemed unapproachable . . . and as for Linzi! She seemed impatient with life, and if cars showed something of their owners, what did a banana-yellow, powerfully noisy car say about Linzi?

Ella smiled. For that matter, what did her elderly, dark-blue, small car say about her? That she was cautious, wanting to merge into the background? With care she could avoid seeing Oliver's owner when she took the dog for walks, and Linzi was only there for weekends and certainly would not come down to Watch Cottage seeking her out.

But who was the mysterious Joel? And why hadn't Audrey mentioned him in her copious notes? Although Ella had been tempted not to move her car just on Linzi's say-so, she had done so. But looking at the turf where it had been parked, she couldn't see what made it different to any other patch. Had Linzi been winding her up?

During that night heavy clouds swept inland obscuring the moon and when Ella woke the room was cold, not even the bright fabrics lifting the gloom. One glance at the billowing slate-grey clouds warned her that bad weather wasn't far away. So after a hurried breakfast, she drove into Clifford, the nearest small town, to stock up with food.

As her car slowly climbed the hill, Ella remembered with a twinge of envy, how easily Linzi's vehicle had soared up it. But reaching the cliff top, the land was flat, tree branches bending away from the coast indicating the ferocity of the sea winds. Clifford was a twenty-minute drive through narrow lanes whose leafless, tall hedges were brightened by sprays of delicate white blackthorn blossom.

Passing a farm whose swinging sign identified it as Peace Farm, which Audrey had mentioned, Ella noticed a roadside board listing produce for sale. When the chimneys of Clifford appeared through gaps in hedges, the road widened, cottages and small houses becoming more frequent.

The car park was nearly full and assuming this was because people had hurried to shop before it rained, Ella went into the main street prepared for packed shops. But to her surprise the pavements were thronged with people staring idly at show windows or going into cafés for coffee, obviously early holidaymakers and visitors.

Ella was pleasantly surprised by the supermarket's varied stock, but after Worcester, the prices were high. She would need to shop carefully for as she was living rent free, Audrey was only paying a small amount to look after Watch Cottage. So guessing vegetables and fruit would be cheaper

13

at Peace Farm, Ella kept her shopping to the minimum.

Out again on the street, she paused to look at a couple of antique shops. In Worcester their contents would not have passed as *antique,* but as well-looked-after old furniture, the sort Audrey had used to furnish Watch Cottage.

When the threatened rain began to fall heavily, Ella hurried back to the car intent on finishing her shopping at the farm, then getting back to the comfort of the cottage.

Peace Farm's produce was sold in a small shed off the yard and as Ella went in, a woman came from the house. But although she was not the picture-book version of a stout, rosy-cheeked country woman, her smile was welcoming.

'You on holiday then?' she asked, weighing out potatoes then helping Ella select carrots and onions.

Her friendliness deserving more than just a 'no', Ella explained she was looking after a cottage.

'That will be Audrey's place and you'll be Ella. I'm Sal. I expect Audrey told you to get your veg from me.'

Ella nodded vaguely, slightly guilty that she hadn't read all the notes.

'Then you'll know to take Will's. Audrey gets fresh stuff for him too. That flighty girl who comes roaring past here at weekends is

14

supposed to bring his shopping, but she'll be into all those faddy diets. Mustn't eat this, mustn't eat that. A man needs to be fed properly, especially when there are bones to mend.'

'But I don't know what he wants.'

'I'll make up the same sort of box Audrey used to take. You don't mind waiting do you? You young girls rush about as though frightened your own shadow will catch you up.'

'No, I don't mind. Can I help?'

'No, perch on that sack of potatoes. It's quite clean.'

And Ella listened to a summary of who lived where, what shops were best in Clifford and how the weather often changed with the tides. When Will's box was packed and Ella asked how much she owed, she was told to pay just for her own things.

'When Will's arm is mended and he can drive again, he'll settle up with me. Mind you give him my best wishes. He needs to concentrate on his new business venture. That girl is supposed to be helping, but I doubt she has one sensible—'

But helping load the car, Sal's last words were more serious. 'And mind you heed what Audrey has told you about Joel. She's told him to keep away but knowing him, it won't make a scrap of difference. But you look sensible enough. Audrey wouldn't have got you if she hadn't thought so, but even the most level-headed can . . . But what am I doing, gossiping like this when you'll be wanting to get home before it really starts raining.'

Although the windscreen wipers were at their highest speed, Ella still had to peer ahead to try keep the car on the narrow lane. If this wasn't what Sal considered to be 'really raining', she would hate to be in a downpour!

Reaching the top of the descent to the bay, Ella stopped, shocked to see water running down the road like a river. Perhaps if she stopped for a few minutes the rain would lessen.

It was when she pulled over by Will's gate that she remembered his box from the farm. She sighed. Would it do tomorrow? But fingers drumming on the steering wheel, she wondered how much food he had in.

What had Sal said about 'bones to be mended'? And if Linzi hadn't brought Will much food . . . Ella shivered with cold and, she realised, hunger. Perhaps Will was hungry too. She was out of the car and battling to open the gate before she had time to reconsider.

Driving up to the cottage, she was surprised to see Oliver run beside the car, obviously very wet. Poor beast, to be out in such weather! What was Will Kennedy thinking about? As she rang the door bell, Oliver danced around, flinging wetness from his shaggy coat over her.

An unexpected strong gust of wind knocking her off balance, she staggered into Will as he opened the door.

'What the . . .?' he exclaimed, as Ella's unexpected weight coupled with Oliver dashing in, sent him against the hall wall.

Regaining his balance, Will opened a door and ordered Oliver into the kitchen. 'Where was Oliver this time? He must have escaped when the postman came.'

'Actually he was in your garden.' Ella's stiff reply hinted that if Will had bothered to look, call, Oliver would have come in.

Sensing this, Will asked sharply, 'So if he was in the garden, what are you doing here? Come to confront his cruel owner?'

'I've brought your veg from the farm.'

Ella hurried back to the car, fighting the wind to shut the boot with one hand as she balanced the box on her hip with the other.

'Here, let me help you . . .' he said, coming towards her.

'Get back inside. I'm already wet,' then following him into the small hall she asked, 'Where shall I put this?'

'I'll take it,' he said, holding out his plastered arm.

'Don't be silly! It's too heavy. You might hurt your arm again.' She squirmed inwardly. Why on earth had she spoken as though to a naughty child?

'I'm not used to being waited on, especially by someone I don't know.'

'We spoke on the phone yesterday. I'm Ella

17

Foulds, so now you know me, please can I put this box down somewhere?'

'Sorry! I'm afraid this arm break seems to have affected my manners. It's so frustrating. No time is ever a "good" time to have an accident, but I could well do without this just now. Oh, the kitchen is behind you.'

Going in, Ella stood frowning. Every flat surface seemed covered with jars, tins, packets of dog food, the sink and draining board a jumble of china and saucepans. It seemed Linzi wasn't very domesticated.

'I'll clear a space on the table.' Embarrassed, Will pushed things together so some were in danger of falling off.

Easing the box down, Ella offered to empty it, put things away. 'No, I can manage,' he replied stiffly.

Cold, wet and suddenly very weary, Ella just nodded as she hurried out, the wind snatching the front door from her, slamming it shut. She didn't feel guilty at the slamming, for the wind had done what she would have liked to do.

It wasn't long before Ella felt warm again, a bowl of hot tomato soup eaten by a roaring fire of driftwood making her feel very relaxed. What a morning it had been. Wild weather, shopping, meeting Sal, then Will. Having just re-read Audrey's notes looking for a mention of Joel, she found none. Nor had Audrey written anything about Will, other than his dog needed walking.

Will had certainly seemed guarded, a little prickly when she'd called with the box, but if this was usual, wouldn't Audrey have warned her?

The phone interrupting her thoughts, she went to answer it, smiling sheepishly. What was she doing thinking so romantically about a man she hardly knew?

'Will Kennedy here. Sorry I was so ungrateful. Thanks for bringing the shopping.'

'It's all right. And I'm sorry I was sharp about Oliver.'

'My fault. I let him out, then forgot. To say I was very busy really is no excuse.'

The silence only lasted a few seconds, but Ella's hand tightened around the phone with awkwardness. Should she say, 'Goodbye'? Put the phone down? But if she did, would it seem as though she hadn't really accepted his apology?

'Ella, did Audrey warn you about . . . Joel?'

'You're the third person who's mentioned Joel. What about him?' she asked sharply, glancing out of the window as though ensuring the mysterious Joel wasn't out there.

'I don't mean to alarm you, but he has a habit of just turning up out of the blue. He's Audrey's nephew. Likes to camp near Watch Cottage. It's just that he "has a way with him", to quote Audrey.'

But before Ella could ask what Audrey might have meant, Will rang off.

CHAPTER THREE

It was the rain rattling against the window
which woke Ella with a start of fright. Where
was she? What was the noise? Throwing back
the duvet she ran to open the curtains,
recoiling as a stormy gust dashed heavy rain
against the glass. But then taking a deep,
calming breath, she realised the cottage was as
steady as a rock.

After the ferocity of the night, the morning
seemed oddly quiet, but although the sun
shone from a duck-egg blue sky, the sea hadn't
settled, white crested waves a reminder of the
storm. Although in the night, Ella had been
grateful for the cottage's snug security, she
hurriedly ate her breakfast, eager to be out
exploring. The spring sun still lacking much
warmth, she pulled on a thick red fleece and
matching cap, both bought for her stay at
Watch Cottage as were the navy, thorn-proof
trousers and walking boots.

Climbing the steep cliff steps up to Will's
cottage, she was glad of sensible clothing,
especially when she stopped a few times to
look at the view and the cold breeze stung her
face. But nearing The Studio, she faltered.
Suppose Oliver wasn't outside as Linzi said he
usually was? What should she say to Will? He
had, though, seemed friendly enough on the

phone . . . And what about the mysterious Joel? Should she ask Will about him?

It was Oliver who put an end to her doubts, for hearing her coming, he barked excitedly, jumping up at the little wooden gate in the wire fence. Exposed to salt-laden wind, the land around The Studio was rough grass, with just a few flowers hugging the shelter of the buildings and arched path.

'Hello, Oliver,' she called out. 'Like a walk?' Then, 'Sssh!' she ordered as his barking became more frenzied. With a wry smile she muttered Linzi's warning under her breath. 'Will must not be disturbed!'

Opening the gate and calming the frolicking dog, Ella was just wondering if she would have to go back down the steps to fetch the lead Audrey kept for him, when Oliver set off around the outside boundary of The Studio. The path was narrow, near the cliff edge so she had to watch where she was going, unlike Oliver who ran ahead, stopping occasionally to check she was following.

'All right, Oliver, you lead the way,' she called out. And lead he did, eventually taking her down to the beach along the steep path, in some places treacherously wet with oozes from the previous night's rain. But once on the firm sand, both Oliver and Ella broke into a run, the dog sometimes dashing into the water. Snatching off her cap, Ella laughed out loud. It was wonderful to feel so carefree.

She had hoped the stay in Watch Cottage would give her time to think about her future. Could she already have the answer? Living close to the sea? A dog for company? But later as she headed back to the cliff steps, she realised dispiritedly she had been carried away by the newness of it all. When Audrey returned, she would have to find a job, somewhere to live. And when Oliver leaned against her as though asking to be stroked, she bit her lip. She would never have thought she could become so fond of a dog in such a short time.

When Ella opened The Studio gate for Oliver, as though sensing her mood, he sat looking at her, his tail for once still.

'It's all right. I'll come for you every day, rain or shine,' she whispered, bending to stroke his damp back. Then, 'Oh dear, you are wet. I shouldn't have let you go in the sea. Perhaps I should offer to dry you. It might be difficult for Will with his right arm in plaster.'

Thirsty after his walk, Oliver broke away to run home where there would be fresh water not tainted by salt. Ella paused briefly, then followed. But when she was a few metres away, she stopped in surprise as Will's door was suddenly opened and she saw him angrily gesticulating to a stout, middle-aged woman. Dressed in smart grey overalls, and baseball cap, she was obviously there to do a job. But what? Ella knew women now trained as plumbers, decorators, electricians . . .

'How many times do you have to be told, I don't need you? I did not book you.' Ella heard Will say.

Then as Oliver tried to jump up at him, Will's annoyance showed in his tone to the dog. 'Sit! I don't want your wetness over me and the house.'

'I'll dry your dog so fast he won't have time to spread the wet. He's sandy too. That can really get into carpets . . .' the woman gabbled.

'No!'

'When you er . . . booked me, she warned you might not take kindly to domestic help. A lot of men don't. It's something to do with their home being their castle . . .'

'She's not my anything. She's . . .'

But then suddenly aware of Ella standing close by, Will took a deep breath, his voice more controlled as he thanked her for taking Oliver for a walk.

'Actually it was he who took me,' she replied lightly. 'Sorry he's wet. Shall I . . . ?'

Suddenly the women bent down and seizing Oliver's collar tried to drag him into the hall. She knew from experience that once she began to clean, even it was only a wet dog, the most difficult of customers were soon making coffee for her. 'It was mentioned I might have to clean up after him.'

Ella heard herself blurting out, 'I'm sorry there seems to be some misunderstanding. I clean for Mr Kennedy, so you're not needed.'

'Why didn't you tell me?' the cleaner snapped at Will. 'I'll need paying for my time.' Glancing at her watch, she made rapid calculations, then added a few pounds, for she guessed Will would not want to prolong the argument in front of the dark-haired girl. 'That will be . . .'

'I'm not giving you a penny. Send your bill to the person who booked you.'

'She said nothing about her paying,' the cleaner said belligerently.

'If I can just get in, I can start,' Ella said to Will with a calmness she wasn't feeling. Why on earth had she said she cleaned for him? But having said it, she might as well act the part. 'Excuse me,' she said. Pushing past the woman, she managed to ease her outside, swiftly shutting the door on her surprised protests.

But if Ella was expecting thanks she soon found Will had no intention of offering them.

'What is it about women that you think men are unable to sort things out for themselves? First Linzi sent that obstinate cleaner without asking me. Then you interfere. A broken arm doesn't mean I'm incapable of fighting my own battles, or for that matter, of looking after myself and my own house.'

In the dim light of the hall Ella looked at him in amazement, rapidly turning to annoyance. 'I was just trying to help. And for

24

your information, I'm nothing like Linzi or that cleaner. As for fighting your own battles, you didn't seem to be doing a very good job. And since you brought up the subject of looking after yourself, from what I saw of your kitchen yesterday . . .'

'You hardly know me so what gives you the right to "help"?'

'By that reckoning I suppose you wouldn't help someone in an accident. After all you wouldn't know them.'

'That's a daft thing to say. Of course I'd help. But I don't need help, Linzi's or yours.'

'Right, in future if you fall down the cliff I'll know not to . . .'

But Ella's acid reply was cut short by Oliver jumping up at Will. Ears flat to his head, tail between his legs, he whined.

'Now you've upset Oliver! He hates loud voices,' Will accused, but quietly.

'Me upset him?' Although her reply was hardly audible, her astonishment was obvious. 'You were shouting at that cleaner as we arrived. If you knew Oliver disliked raised voices, why didn't you calm down when you saw him?'

'I . . . Oh I don't know why.' Then, 'Yes I do! Organising women . . .'

'Will, stop please!' Ella raised her hands as though fending off anything which might start them arguing again. 'I think I'd better go.'

Stooping she patted the dog, whispering just

loud enough for Will to hear, 'You've been a very good boy!'

Instead of going back down the steps, Ella followed the twisting steep road, for in her present confused frame of mind, she didn't trust herself to safely negotiate the steep steps. What had happened to the lovely day? She had felt so happy walking Oliver. But that had all been shattered by Will.

To try to stop the whirl of thoughts which centred around Will and his seeming dislike of her, Ella spent the afternoon working hard. Surprised that the wind-whipped sea had flung up so much rubbish onto the beach, she filled bin bags with plastic bottles, rope, punctured balls, odd shoes, plastic crates. Why, she thought, couldn't people take their rubbish home? Or keep it on board ship?

She was pleased to see a lot of wood and as she carried or dragged the large pieces back to the cottage, she hoped the summer sun would dry those which were damp. It would be nice to surprise Audrey with a good supply. Ella firmly banished the thought that with Audrey's return, she would have to leave. She still had nearly six months to think what she would do with her life.

CHAPTER FOUR

After spending much of the next morning mulling over the various scenarios which might greet her when she went for Oliver, it was afternoon before Ella climbed the cliff steps. Nearing the top step, she saw fastened to the gate a white envelope with Ella scrawled right across it.

To her surprise it was a silent Oliver who was waiting for her, but his tail was wagging furiously. Letting him out, she smiled wryly, It was as though the dog knew not to alert his master of her arrival. Not even glancing towards The Studio in case she saw Will, she concentrated on freeing the envelope as though the slightest tear would be a disaster. Then thrusting it into her fleece pocket, she hurried after Oliver.

She knew Will might think it childish of her, not reading his note, but she was proving to herself that he was really not all that important. Instead, she fixed her thoughts on the early sea pinks bending against the wind . . . Oliver . . . a small fishing boat bobbing up and down . . .

It wasn't until she reached an outcrop of dove-grey rocks on the shore that slipping her hand in her pocket, she fingered the envelope. With a sigh, she took out the short typed note.

Ella, I can't apologise enough for my appalling behaviour yesterday! To say I dislike being organised sounds very weak and I'm sorry you were caught up in my annoyance about the cleaning woman. I'm writing this in the hope you will still be taking Oliver for his daily walk. If you do, please call in when you bring him back. Perhaps we could have a cup of coffee? Start again . . . Yours abjectly, Will.

His signature was badly scrawled, perhaps, Ella thought, because he had used his left hand. Hugging her knees against the cold breeze, she appeared to be watching Oliver, but her eyes were unfocused as though looking inwards at her thoughts. What should she do? Certainly Will had apologised. But suppose not enough time had elapsed for their hot words to have cooled completely?

She would have to watch what she said and this might make her seem aloof, unforgiving . . . But on the other hand not accepting Will's invitation might make any future contact between them, however brief, stilted, and that was no way to foster neighbourliness.

A sudden cold shiver made her look out to sea. A grey veil of drizzle was advancing inland. Time to go, if she wasn't to get a wetting. Calling Oliver, she hurried back up the cliff path, arriving at Will's gate hot and out of breath just as clinging drizzle enveloped her.

'Ella, come in and shelter!' Will called from

the doorway. 'I know from bitter experience this mizzle can drench you in no time at all.'

Glancing back, Ella could see nothing clearly, the mizzle, as Will had called it, was so heavy. So as Oliver ran towards the cottage, she joined him, arriving breathless at the door.

'Come in,' Will invited standing aside to allow her to enter. Then, 'Oliver . . . Kitchen!' he ordered. As the dog obeyed, Will said with a smile, 'We'd better go there too. It's warm with the Aga and I have tidied!"

Deliberately Ella kept her eyes fixed on Oliver lying in front of the Aga, licking the moisture from his coat.

'Don't you believe I've tidied?' Will asked with a laugh.

Glancing around, Ella replied, 'My goodness, you really have! It must have been difficult with your arm in plaster.'

'Although I'm not naturally left-handed, it's surprising what you can do when pushed.'

'Who pushed you?' she asked lightly. Was Linzi there? Would she appear, smiling slightly at Ella's dishevelled state?

But ignoring her question, Will held out his hand. 'Come on, let me have your fleece. It will soon dry by the Aga.'

As she handed it to him, Ella wondered why he hadn't answered her question. Was it because having said he disliked organising women, he didn't want to admit that his new found tidiness had indeed been precipitated by

Linzi?

Crouching to stroke Oliver, she asked him if he had been the one to instigate the clearing up.

'No,' Will replied. 'But Oliver does make some of the mess. He's not a neat eater and he's beginning to moult. Actually, it was that cleaning woman. I think my temper flared because deep down I knew the place was a tip.'

'And then I came along and made matters worse. I'm sorry . . .' Giving Oliver one last pat, Ella stood up. Then wanting to change the subject, she reminded, 'I could really do with that coffee.'

'I know I rather jumped the gun, but the percolator is ready, it just needs switching on. But perhaps you could try opening the biscuit tin? When Linzi was last here, she jammed the lid so I can't get it off.'

Picking up the round tin decorated with purple thistles, Ella bit her lip with the effort of prising off the lid. 'My goodness, was she trying to stop you eating biscuits?' she asked. Then as the lid suddenly came off, she just managed to prevent the contents from spilling out.

'He's one of the reasons,' Will said, nodding towards Oliver. 'He's got a sweet tooth and Linzi says he's too fat. Me too, since I stopped work.'

He asked her to pass him two mugs hanging on hooks under a shelf.

As she complied, Ella saw Will was smiling, not only with his mouth, but with his eyes. What a startling blue they were. Summer-skies-blue . . .

'A penny for your thoughts?'

'I . . . I was wondering if I offered you and Oliver a biscuit, would Linzi come after me?'

'I won't tell her if you won't,' Will said to the dog as he gave him a biscuit. 'These are Sal's home made cherry ones and we both like them.'

'But seriously, I have put on weight since I stopped working fourteen hours a day, six days a week for Linzi's father. Not that he has asked me to. But he's always been good to me . . . Then of course this happened,' he said, indicating the plaster. 'Let's sit down. Try the rocking chair. It was Audrey's housewarming present to me.'

Leaning back in it, Ella set it in gentle motion, cradling her mug in her hands to stop it slopping.

'Did your accident stop you working for him?' she asked.

'No. Like many others, I suddenly got tired trying to please dissatisfied clients forever changing their minds, wanting things done yesterday . . .'

'What did you do?'

'Linzi's father is a property developer, a builder, and lucky for me, he's also my godfather. When I didn't know what to do

31

when I left university with a computer degree and absolutely no desire to spend my life doing that sort of thing, he offered me a job. Taught me so much. He's the most generous of men.'

'So you've always known Linzi?'

When his, 'Yes,' was exhaled on a sigh, Ella risked looking at him, but his face was expressionless. Quickly he asked, 'Why are you looking after Audrey's cottage? Are you an amateur artist seeking inspiration?'

Shaking her head, she replied the only brush she was any good with was a large one for decorating. 'I really enjoy it. I've done a lot at home, my parents' home that is.'

She didn't see Will's slight frown when she had corrected to, 'my parents' home'. Hadn't she been happy there? Where exactly was 'home' for Ella?

'Audrey said you'd worked in an office . . .' Although the atmosphere was relaxed, Ella didn't want to tell him she was hoping the six months at Watch Cottage would give her the chance to think about a new career. But before she could turn the conversation away from herself, Will suddenly got up and hurried to the window.

'Blast! I might have guessed he would turn up now.'

Putting her feet on the floor to stop the rocking chair, Ella stood up, reaching for her coat. 'If you've a visitor . . .'

'It's not me who has the visitor. It's you, and

an unwelcome one too.'

'But no-one knows I'm here.'

'I wouldn't be surprised if Joel does know you're here,' Will said tight-lipped. It's just what he'd do, despite Audrey telling him she'd let you have the cottage.'

'But how do you know it's him? I didn't think you could see into the bay from your windows.'

'I've a good ear for car engines.'

'I'd better go then. Thanks for the coffee and for drying me out. Joel might want something. Audrey's address perhaps.'

'I doubt it. He's a wanderer. Comes and goes as the mood suits him. Stays for a few days then . . .'

'Stays?' she repeated, appalled.

With a wintry smile Will reassured, 'It's all right. He always pitches a tent. He carries it around with him, says it's useful if he has to wait about for a special effect like a sunrise, or moonlight on the sea. He's a landscape photographer. A good one to give him his due. No doubt he'll ask you to watch the moon with him.' Then, 'Ella . . .' Two long strides took him directly in front of her and cupping her chin in his hand, he looked at her seriously. 'Joel can't resist a pretty face.'

He had only held her for a second but to Ella it seemed like an eternity. It was she though who broke the spell. 'I'd better go!'

CHAPTER FIVE

Ella went down the cliff steps faster than was sensible on the wet surface, unaware that Will was standing by the little gate, watching her. If she had known his brooding thoughts, that her speed was in eagerness to meet Joel, she might have slowed down.

But Ella's haste was to do with a man. Not Joel. Will! She was trying to suppress the bubble of elation caused by his words.

As she reached the bottom step, Joel walked lazily towards her. But his eyes weren't lazy, he was scrutinising her intently. Hands in pockets of worn orange cords, his T-shirt a vivid mauve, dark brown curls, shoulder length, her first thought was that he deliberately cultivated an artistic look. Shorter than Will, and stockier, he still moved with the controlled certainty of a cat.

'Hi! You must be Audrey's cottage keeper. Lucky cottage!'

Remembering Will's warning, her smile was thinly polite. 'I don't know if Audrey told you my name . . .' When he shook his head, she held out her hand, 'I'm Ella Foulds.' She hoped this formality would tell him that he might know Audrey, but this did not give him any rights as far as she, Ella, was concerned.

Glancing to where a big four-wheel drive

vehicle stood on what she had come to think of 'as sacred turf', she added, 'I was warned you always parked there.'

'Who by? I can't imagine it was Audrey.' He was blocking her way, eyes narrowed as though trying to fathom what else might have been said about him.

'It was Linzi,' she replied, sidestepping to go purposefully towards Watch Cottage.

'Linzi? Is she here?' he asked, long strides bringing him level.

'She came down when I first arrived.' At the door, Ella took the large key from her pocket, but his watchful nearness made her clumsy.

'Here, let me,' he said, taking the key from her. 'I keep telling Audrey she should have a new lock fitted with a more manageable key.' Although he opened the door wide, he moved sideways into the space, partially blocking her way. 'I expect she warned *you* off Will.'

'Who? Audrey?'

'No, Linzi. She regards him as her personal property.'

'Actually she came here looking for Oliver. That's all. Now, if you'll let me pass . . .'

'Certainly, if it means you'll offer me a cup of tea, or better still a meal. I've driven a long way without a break.'

'Suppose I'd not been here? Away for the day? What would you have done for food then?' she questioned, kicking off her boots by the door.

'Gone back into Clifford. But,' he smiled winningly. 'I knew Audrey wouldn't have let anyone hard-hearted look after her precious cottage. She usually feeds me. Didn't she tell you?' As though this gave him the right to enter, he too kicked off boots, worn ones of suede.

'No and I'm not . . .'

But Ella's reply that she wasn't Audrey was cut short by rain against the small windows. The kitchen suddenly darkened by black clouds, Ella switched on the light. Turning round, she saw Joel's tiredness, the droop of his shoulders, dark shadows under his eyes.

'I haven't got all that much in,' she said, taking off her fleece. Normally it was hung behind the door, but Joel was standing there so instead she dropped it on a chair. Pushing up the sleeves of her emerald sweater she busied herself fetching pasta from a cupboard, a saucepan from a shelf. 'While I'm cooking, would you light the fire in the living room.' It was not a question, more of an order and this surprised her almost as much as it did him.

But Joel didn't go immediately. 'I didn't have you down as a girl who would go for such a vivid colour as that sweater.'

'I don't. It was a leaving present from the girls I shared a flat with. They thought I needed brightening up.'

Although busy preparing the cheese sauce for the pasta, Ella was listening to the sounds of newspaper being scrunched up, kindling laid, a few matches being struck, then after a few minutes, more substantial wood being taken from the log basket. So far so good. He was leaving her alone.

'Right. Now, what can I do?'

She thought she would hear him when he came back into the kitchen, but as a landscape photographer not wanting to scare wildlife, he knew how to move silently. Startled, she dropped the bread knife she was using on the floor.

'You are jumpy, aren't you?' he said, bending to pick it up. Rinsing the knife under the tap, then drying it, he handed it back to her. Briefly smiling her thanks, Ella was relieved he hadn't taken the opportunity to touch her hand. 'Perhaps it's just as well I'm here to protect you. It's lonely here and there are sudden storms . . .'

'I can look after myself,' she retorted, vigorously slicing the loaf.

'I can see that from the way you're wielding that knife. Heaven help any intruder . . .'

Intent on putting bread slices on a plate, she spoke briskly. 'If you've been here before you'll know where Audrey keeps the cutlery so please lay the table in there,' she indicated the living room with a nod of her head.

'Audrey always ate at the kitchen table.'

'I prefer the living room.'

Ella didn't tell him that by eating in the

relative formality of the other room she would hopefully be indicating that this meal was not the prelude for others. This was strictly a one-off!

'I never could understand why Audrey preferred to eat in the kitchen when the table by the living room window has such a splendid sea view. But you obviously do appreciate it.'

Although Ella took a deep breath as though to reply, she said nothing. Why was it everything Joel said made her want to respond with something sharp, clever? She might have got off to a bad start with Will, but talking to him was far easier.

As she served the pasta, Joel peered out of the window then with a muttered, 'Good, the rain is slackening!' ran to his vehicle, returning with a bottle of red wine.

Going to a small oak corner cupboard, he took out two beautifully-engraved wine glasses and putting them on the table, uncorked the wine.

As they sat down at the small table, his foot touched hers and she shifted slightly away. 'Sorry!' Sliding a speculative look in her direction, he added, 'Audrey is right. There is more room at the kitchen table.'

But Ella didn't reply, instead concentrating on her food.

'Here's to us then!' When he raised his glass in her direction, although flustered by the 'us', Ella responded. Putting down her glass, she offered the plate of bread, indicating butter and also margarine.

'How did you know I preferred butter?' he drawled. 'Did Audrey leave a list of my likes and dislikes?'

'It might surprise you to know she didn't write, or say, a single word about you. And as for having both butter and margarine, I prefer butter on toast, marg on sandwiches.'

Joel was indeed hungry for instead of the smart reply she expected, he was silent as he ate. Although when preparing the food, Ella had also felt hungry, sitting with Joel, her appetite vanished.

'You're not eating much,' he observed. 'Are you dieting, or am I putting you off?'

'Neither, I had a large lunch,' she lied.

'In that case it was kind of you to make this,' he said indicating his empty plate. 'It was the best pasta I've tasted for ages.'

'You said Audrey always gave you a meal . . .' Deliberately Ella used the singular 'meal'. As far as she was concerned she would not be providing any more meals!

Waiting for him to reply, she sipped her wine, trying to hide a slight shudder. But he didn't reply, seeming intent at gazing out of the window. But what could he see? The dark clouds had brought on an early twilight. 'You seem to know her well . . .'

'She's my aunt,' he replied shortly, getting up from the table. Thanking her again, he added it was time he pitched his tent.

'Has it stopped raining?' Ella cringed inwardly, appalled at her question. To a man like Joel it might seem like an invitation to sleep in the cottage and although the old sofa would be long enough for him, there was no way she wanted him, or anyone else to sleep there. But to her relief, Joel said he was used to being in the tent in all weathers, had all the right sleeping equipment so was very comfortable.

When he had gone, Ella carefully turned the door key, hoping Joel wouldn't hear its squeaky protest. She didn't want him thinking she was afraid of him. But up in her bedroom, craning her neck to see his tent, she had to admit that she was indeed a little afraid of him. But not for one moment did she think he would harm her physically. It was more subtle than that.

She might only have been with him for a short time, but a sixth sense warned he might harm her emotions. Turning *away* from the window, she told herself she was being silly, was being influenced by what Linzi, Sal and Will had said. And when she really considered it, what had they really said? Nothing really.

Hunched in a coat, the right, empty sleeve hanging limply, Will looked down at the bay, and seeing Joel pitch his tent, he nodded, satisfied. There would be no cosy chatting around Ella's fire until the small hours. But he

40

brushed aside the thought that he didn't mind at all when Linzi spent hours talking to Joel when he visited Audrey. Linzi could take care of herself. Ella though . . . What on earth was the matter with him? He hardly knew her.

CHAPTER SIX

Opening her curtains with the dawn, Ella was surprised to see Joel's vehicle had gone, but his tent was still there. Wondering if he had left a note, she showered and dressed quickly, but the little wooden box for post outside the door was empty. She quelled the slight feeling of disappointment by reminding herself sharply that there was absolutely no reason for him to tell her where he was going.

Breakfasting and tidying up while the washing machine was on, she then hung the washing on the whirly line tucked behind the cottage, but even here the wind was strong enough to send it spinning vigorously. Hands on hips she waited for a little while to see everything was securely pegged, then glancing at her watch, sighed. It was still only nine o'clock! But remembering she was nearly out of milk, she decided to see if Sal sold any.

Ella had no intention of calling on Will, after all, she had seen him the previous day. Her car though seemed to go of its own accord

41

in front of his gate. Will had recognised the sound of her car engine, Oliver was at the opening of the gate, then Ella's footsteps, so she was greeted by them both.

'I wasn't expecting you, but it seems Oliver was,' he laughed, pointing to the dog cavorting around her. 'Everything all right?' Head on one side, he looked at her keenly.

'Yes, why shouldn't it be?' she replied abruptly, bending to fondle Oliver's floppy ears.

'Your visitor . . . ?'

'Has gone out.' Then standing up, she looked directly at Will, almost daring him to ask any more questions about Joel. 'I'm going to Peace Farm. Do you want anything? I'm hoping they sell milk.'

'Yes, Sal does, not from her own cows though. They went during the foot and mouth outbreak a few years ago and it so took the heart out of her and her husband, that when the time came for them to restock, they decided not to. So for the convenience of customers, she takes a few bottles from another farm. But thanks, Linzi brought me some and she'll be coming again at the weekend.'

Ella turned to leave, but Oliver got in her way and she would have fallen if Will hadn't caught and steadied her. But ordering Oliver to lie down, he kept his arm around Ella's shoulder.

'Sorry about him tripping you up, but he thinks you're going to take him for a walk.'

'Perhaps I will, then go for milk.' Although Will's arm was only resting lightly on her, she was totally unprepared for how she was feeling. She hadn't thought Will the sort of man to maintain physical contact, however innocent. She wanted to shake herself free, but . . . it was comforting . . .

'If you don't mind dogs in your car, you could take Oliver with you. He's very good, lies down on the back seat. Then if you want to, you can walk around Sal's fields. I often do that when I'm working there.'

Sure, she was blushing like a child. Ella would have agreed to anything to have a reason for moving away from Will's arm. And Oliver helped, for seeing Will's gesture for him to get up, he rushed to the gate with Ella running after him.

At Peace Farm, Ella left Oliver in the car, but when Sal came from the house and saw him, she opened the car door, the dog nearly knocking her over as he jumped up.

'Oliver, get down!' Ella commanded with no effect.

'It's all right. He and I are good friends. I only have an old dog now, so it's good to have a boisterous dog about the place. Now, what can I get you?'

Ella's purchases of milk and cheese were quickly done, and although Sal was pleasant, it

43

was obvious she didn't want to gossip. But when Ella asked if she could take Oliver around the fields, Sal indicated a gate across the yard, saying Oliver knew which way he normally went with Will.

Pausing occasionally to check Ella was following, Oliver ran around the field edge, stopping when a particular interesting smell caught his attention. Watching him, Ella thought it was a pity he couldn't tell her what was so intriguing. Had a badger trundled along during the night? A fox been hunting?

Jumping over stiles with ease, Oliver waited with tail-wagging impatience for her to clamber over. They soon reached a compromise, she stopping whilst he investigated a particularly intriguing smell or noise, then he sat patiently when she stood admiring the view or twigs of yellow catkins bobbing like lambs tails.

It was only when she heard the sound of a car that Ella realised they were near the road and this was borne out when the last stile took them on to a stoned lane which she presumed led to the road down to the bay. She hesitated, wondering whether to return the same way, but Oliver was running off down the lane.

'Oliver! Stop!' she ordered, frowning as the normally obedient dog ignored her. Instead he was standing by a tall, uncut hawthorn hedge, tail wagging.

With a sigh she went to him, hoping he

hadn't found an injured animal or bird. But as she went up to him she saw he was standing expectantly by a wooden gate leading to a cottage, which from the piles of old wood and bricks in the overgrown garden, was unoccupied.

'Do you want to go in then?' Ella asked the dog, although she knew it was her own curiosity which wanted to peep through the windows. Although an empty cottage or house could look desolate, there was an air of mystery about them she couldn't resist. They carried nothing of the character of previous owners, but glimpsing rooms she could try to imagine what they had been like, what she could do with the interiors.

The cottage's roof was tiled and by the look of it, had recently been repaired. Going up the short path it was obvious it had been used, for there were wheel marks of a wheelbarrow, footprints in the unmown grass. Either side of the front door there was a small window and going up to one, Ella cupped her hands, all the better to see in. The skirting boards had been stripped of paint, the paperless walls repaired and from the pile of old wallpaper in the middle of the room, it seemed the previous occupant had liked large red roses.

A staircase rose from the back of the room, presumably to the bedrooms, whose small windows were tucked under the roof eaves. Going to the window on the other side of the front door, Ella saw tins of emulsion and one wall had been emulsioned in a pale straw colour. The back wall had a small hatch and guessing this linked with the kitchen at the back, Ella was just going round to try to see it, when Oliver growled.

'My goodness, Will has got you working for him quickly. First Linzi, now you.'

Recognising Joel's voice, she turned to see him sauntering up the path. To her surprise, Oliver was still growling and fearing he might become aggressive, she took hold of his collar.

'That apology for a dog has never liked me, nor Linzi for that matter. I would have said he was a one man dog, but I see he likes you. Now I wonder why?' Joel's eyes held hers as though trying to read her thoughts.

Still holding Oliver, Ella countered with, 'What are you doing here?'

'I would have thought it was obvious,' he replied, lifting his camera. But there was something in his half smile which warned he knew something she did not and he was going to take pleasure in telling her.

'You didn't know this was Will's flight of fancy, did you? Did that wretched dog bring you here?'

'What do you mean "flight of fancy"?' Ella asked.

'Hasn't he told you? Now, I wonder why not? Perhaps because it's his and Linzi's precious secret. Will has thrown caution to the winds and thinks he can make a fortune by doing up old dumps like this, then letting them as holiday cottages.'

'That seems perfectly reasonable to me,' Ella replied. 'But this cottage is hardly a "dump". It looks to have been well restored.'

'I suppose, if you like that sort of thing . . . I prefer a five star hotel.'

'Is that what you call your tent?' There was a tart edge to her question which she couldn't understand. Why did Joel's opinion of Will's cottage matter?

Nodding to say he understood her barb, Joel waved his hand at the cottage. 'I suppose it might look better when Linzi gets going with her eye for the latest in interior design. Oh dear, I hope Will hadn't led you to believe you could . . .'

'Will hasn't led me to believe anything. I came here by chance and what Will and Linzi do is none of my business. But you haven't answered my question. What are you doing here? Has Will asked you to take photographs of the cottage?'

'Me, take photos of holiday lets,' he said disparagingly. 'Landscapes, that's my claim to fame. Haven't you ever read about my exhibitions? No, I don't suppose you would.'

'Exactly what do you mean by that?' Ella asked coldly. 'That I'm too stupid?'

'Oh come on, don't tell me the sea breezes has blown away your sense of humour . . .'

47

'They've obviously blown away any tact you might have had.' Then still holding Oliver's collar, Ella left.

It was lunch time when she let the weary dog out of the car and back into Will's garden. She watched him go towards the door of the small building, saw him scratch to be let in.

Hearing the door open she began to smile in readiness to say something to Will. But the door closed quickly. Surely Will must have guessed she would watch Oliver go in? She frowned.

It was almost as though he didn't want to see her. As though he knew she had been to the renovated cottage.

Although tired and hungry, she drove slowly down to Watch Cottage, not because of Will, but Joel. Would his vehicle be there? She hoped not, she'd had enough of him for one day. She loved the peace and quiet of the bay, but Joel camping close by was having an unsettling effect on her. When she could see the whole bay, she breathed a sigh of relief. Joel hadn't returned.

Before going indoors, she went to check her washing was dry and as she removed the pegs, she paused. Why had she been disappointed that Will hadn't at least waved to her? Dropping the washing into the plastic laundry basket, a reason flashed through her thoughts, but swiftly she banished it.

CHAPTER SEVEN

Typically April weather, what had begun as a fine day ended with harsh showers. When the wind rose, cresting the waves with white, Ella ran up to her bedroom window to peer down at Joel's tent. She had never camped so didn't know if the tent was secure.

Although presuming Joel would soon return, niggles of worry about his tent persisted and to still them, she decided to make a chicken casserole, large enough for two days. Putting it in the oven she tried to settle down to read, putting on the radio to try to deaden the blustery wind.

She had managed to read a few chapters when a particularly savage gust rattled the windows. Opening the door just sufficiently to look at the tent, she ducked back inside, biting her lip with worry. Should tents be flat like that? Scrambling into waterproofs, she opened the door, gasping as the wind tore it from her.

Head bent she circled the tent, but looking at the ropes and pegs she hesitated to touch them even though the whole thing seemed to be leaning. Suppose by trying to tighten a rope she did something silly and the whole lot blew away?

But what was that bright yellow shape, blurred by the rain? Pulling her hood tighter to shield her eyes a little, she realised the blur was moving, coming down the hill. Something must have happened to Joel's vehicle, so he was walking. Knowing the back of Watch Cottage would offer shelter, Ella flattened herself against the wall, shoulders hunched against the drips coming from the low roof.

She didn't see Oliver until she was sent staggering by his enthusiastic greeting. 'Oliver what are you doing out in this?' she gasped.

'I could ask you the same question.' The words were distorted by a gust of wind but she recognised Will's voice. Dressed in yellow oilskins, she was so relieved to see him she put her hand on his left arm.

'The tent . . . Joel isn't here . . .'

'I realised that when I went to fetch Oliver in and looked down here. Then I saw you struggling . . . Look, can you give me a hand to secure it more firmly? This accursed plaster restricts my movements, makes me ham-fisted. But first, could you put Oliver inside? Weather like this makes him excited and he might do something daft.'

Working under Will's skilful directions, they soon secured the tent more firmly. 'Right,' he mouthed at her, the wind blowing his words away. 'I'll get Oliver now.'

But when they went in, Oliver did not come to greet them in his usual exuberant way, he was stretched out in front of the living-room fire.

Aware the rain was running off his waterproof, Will stayed on the tiled kitchen floor as he encouraged, 'Come on boy, home!' But he was ignored.

'It's very wild outside. Perhaps Oliver has the right idea,' Ella said, shrugging off her coat. She didn't look at Will as she asked, 'Would you like to stay until it calms down?' Then remembering the casserole, she added, 'I've enough chicken casserole in the oven for two if you're prepared to wait until it's ready.'

When Will didn't reply, but looked from Oliver to the rain-washed window, she wished she hadn't asked. 'It certainly smells good,' Will said. 'But when Joel comes back . . .'

Realising Will had thought she had cooked the meal for Joel, Ella half laughed as she explained the large quantity was to save her cooking the next day, not for Joel. Then hopping about on one leg as she got out of the waterproof trousers, she added, 'I am not about to provide a restaurant service for him.' Then remembering she had indeed given Joel a meal, she became even more awkward and would have fallen, if Will hadn't caught her.

'Thanks,' she muttered, turning slightly so she was free of his hand. 'Look, how about you getting out of those wet things and keeping Oliver company whilst I set the table.'

Glancing at him, she saw from his raised eyebrows and slight smile that he realised she had deliberately freed herself. What must he think of her behaving like a silly schoolgirl?

Although he was a little awkward getting out of his wet outer clothing, there was a look of grim determination on his face which told her it would be unwise to offer help. But instead of going into the living-room, he fetched cutlery and without asking, laid the kitchen table.

Bending to get the casserole out of the oven, Ella heard Oliver's claws on the tiled floor, but he stood well away, sniffing the aroma.

'Can I give him some?' she asked Will, who had put a board on the table for the hot dish.

'No doubt he would enjoy it. Audrey though usually had a tin or two of dog food for him under the sink and his bowl is there too. But perhaps a bit of gravy over it . . . ?'

Sifting down at the kitchen table Ella felt ill at ease. It was too homely . . . too intimate. But why should this worry her? After all, it was obvious Will often had a meal with Audrey. Both hungry and still a little chilled, they ate in silence. Will did not need much persuasion to finish the last of the casserole and finding she was watching him, looking at the way his fair hair was catching the light, the way he was so at ease, she hurriedly asked him about the little cottage he was renovating.

'Oh, you've seen it. Did Sal tell you about it?' he asked, pushing away his empty plate with a contented sigh.

'No, it was Oliver who led me there and then Joel came by . . .'

'And no doubt told you how stupid I was to give up a good job.'

Ella replied obliquely, 'Is he perhaps regretting he hasn't a proper job?'

'For goodness sake don't say that to him! Joel wouldn't want to do anything other than photography, and in all fairness, he is good. But like all artistic pursuits, it doesn't put much jam on his bread. He's planning an exhibition in a small local gallery. When it's on, would you like to go with me?' he asked. Then added ruefully, 'That is if I'm free of this plaster by then.'

'In that case, if you don't mind being driven by a woman, we can go in my car.'

'I guess you wouldn't drive as though the devil was chasing you, like Linzi does.'

'If I had her car I might be less cautious. Mine is more sedate, like me.'

'No, not sedate. Reliable,' Will said softly.

Glancing up at him, Ella saw he was looking thoughtful as though he was wondering why he had said 'reliable'.

'But I guess that's why Audrey got you to look after her home. She loves this place, put her heart and soul into repairing it and buying the right sort of furniture.'

'Like you're doing with your cottage?' Ella asked, elbows on the table, cupped hands framing her face.

She didn't realise how earnest she looked, interested in what he might be doing. After a moment's pause, Will responded slowly, quietly, as though half afraid Ella would interrupt with her own ideas.

'I'm going to keep the cottage simple, but comfortably furnished. Holidaymakers don't want to be watching children to see they don't damage things, or feeling the place is so upmarket that it isn't like home, they can't relax. The cottage won't sleep more than two adults and two children and the kitchen is small, but I hope to fit a dishwasher, for washing up is a chore at the best of times.

'And the decorating and furniture?'

'Linzi thinks my ideas are too "countrified" as she calls it.'

Sitting up straight, Ella glanced around Audrey's cosy kitchen, then indicating the living-room, she asked, 'I like this. Do you?'

His vigorous nod was all she needed to continue, 'Then why not do as you want to. After all it is to be your business and you want people to come back again, recommend others.'

'Yes, yes I will!'

The determination is both his voice and expression made Ella smile, but not for long. Suddenly the door was flung open and Joel came in. Throwing back the hood of his waterproof, he saw Will and Ella. For a fleeting second Ella saw an expression on his face which sent a chill down her spine.

But when he spoke, it was jokingly, teasing.

'So what have we here? A cosy twosome. How romantic. When Ella made me a meal, we sat more formally in the living-room.'

'I wouldn't have called it "formal",' Ella said, standing. 'If you're coming in or going out, then please shut the door. The wind is lowering the temperature.' And it wasn't only the temperature in the room which had chilled she observed.

'Ella,' Will began hurriedly. 'I think it's time I went.'

But then Oliver ran from the other room to stand by Ella, barking loudly.

'How interesting. That's twice that mutt of yours has taken on the role of defending Ella, though on neither occasion was it necessary. He doesn't seem to be so protective of Linzi. I wonder why? They say animals have a sixth sense. Is he in some way picking up something from you Will, about your feelings?'

'As usual you're talking a load of rubbish,' was the gruff reply. 'By the way, you should secure your tent better if you don't want it blown away. Ella and I've done the best we can. I hope you have a comfortable night.'

'Is that your way of telling me to go? I'm sorry if I'm in the way, interrupted something.'

Annoyed both by the way she was being ignored and by Joel's hint that she and Will had been up to goodness knows what, Ella spoke with an authority which surprised her. 'Please go, both of you. I came here for peace and quiet, not to have a verbal brawl disturbing it.'

With an abject smile of apology, Will did not bother to put on his waterproofs and seeing this Ella spoke without thinking. 'Will, do put on your waterproofs. I know it's not raining quite as much but the wind is strong.'

'How touching,' Joel remarked. 'Are you going to show me the same concern, Ella?'

Her only reply was to point at the door and with a shrug, Joel left.

CHAPTER EIGHT

'Any chance of breakfast?' This time Joel did knock briefly before opening the door, coming just far enough in to be able to shut it. Coupled with a disturbed night Ella answered sharply, continuing to eat her boiled egg. 'I am not running a café!'

'Oh dear, are you still mad with me about teasing Will last night? Look,' suddenly serious he moved towards her, but one look at Ella's face made him stop. 'I really am sorry about it. Will and I just seem to rub each other up the wrong way. I shouldn't have used you as ammunition. It was unfair of me. My only excuse and it's a feeble one, is that Linzi doesn't mind me having a go at him. In fact she joins in!'

Her egg finished, Ella flattened the empty shell with several sharp taps with her spoon.

Pretending to wince, Joel smiled disarmingly. 'Could that be me you're attacking?'

'I always do that,' Ella said, standing to clear the table. 'It stops witches using the empty shell as a boat. That's what my grandmother told me and old habits die hard.'

'So in that case will you forgive my bad habit of getting at Will?' Joel asked softly. 'He and I were at school together, he was always better than me in just about everything. And if I'm being perfectly honest, everything seems to fall the right way for him. He got into university, I didn't. He got a good degree, but then decided he didn't want to continue with computers. Then Linzi's father offered him a job . . . But not content with that, Will decides to try something else. Then there's Linzi . . .'

Whilst Joel had been speaking, Ella had seemingly been busy putting away the marmalade, butter and milk. But she had heard every word and was astonished. Joel had seemed so self-assured. But perhaps beneath that happy-go-lucky exterior he was just as uncertain about life as she was.

'I'd better go before I tell you my boring life story.'

'I'd like to know about your photography,'

she said. 'And as I don't want you collapsing with hunger, would you like bacon and egg?'

Ella sat opposite Joel at the kitchen table as he ate, then talked. She was surprised when the living-room clock chimed ten times. Once he realised Ella's interest was genuine, Joel's obvious enthusiasm for landscape photography had her asking questions which he answered, showing great patience as she struggled to understand some technicality.

He too heard the clock and pushing back his chair, apologised for being a bore.

'You haven't bored me at all,' Ella replied as he stood up. 'And as for feeling . . . well sort of . . .' she just stopped herself from saying, 'jealous of Will,' she continued hastily, 'Joel, I might not know anything about your photography, your reputation, but it seems to me you're obviously good at what you do and it's clear you enjoy it.'

'And you Ella, what do you enjoy doing?' he asked softly.

Flustered, she too stood up but as she reached forward to clear the table, he took hold of her hands. When he looked at her searchingly, she was silent, confused both by his question and his quiet sincerity.

'Well?' Gently he jiggled her hands up and down as though trying to shake the answer from her.

When she shook her head several times and sighed, he added softly, 'Ella, whatever you've come here to find, I hope you do.'

He left with just a wave of thanks towards the breakfast table. Following him to the door, she did not immediately close it, but watched him walk purposefully to his vehicle. But it wasn't Joel she was thinking about, it was Will. It had taken several attempts for him to find what he wanted to do, rescue old cottages to turn into pretty holiday lets. And from what Joel had said, she felt he would never swap his photography for anything else. In their different ways they were lucky to be doing what . . .

'Pull yourself together, Ella,' she suddenly exclaimed out loud. After all she had only been at Watch Cottage for a few days. There was plenty of time for her to decide what she wanted to do.

*   *   *

As Joel drove away, Ella stood on the shingle which separated sand from turf. It was surprisingly warm, such a marked contrast from the rain and wind of the previous day. Lifting her face to the sun she marvelled at such a change, but April was a skittish month switching from rain to sunshine with startling rapidity. The incoming tide was gentle, the sea so calm, that at times it mirrored the blobs of white clouds.

Looking at the coastline, she realised she

still hadn't explored beyond the cliffs which sheltered the furthest side of Watch Cottage. So she decided to pack a few sandwiches and make a day of it.

Her small backpack holding all she needed, Ella scrambled over the tumble of rocks which had fallen from the sheer cliff face. Rounding the cliff edge away from what she now thought of as 'her bay', she paused. Ahead rose sheer cliffs as far as she could see.

Her socks and walking shoes left with her backpack, she wandered from pool to pool, standing in the bigger ones, shuddering with the coldness of the water, but yet enjoying it. The raucous screech of the gulls didn't mar the silence, they were so much a part of the seaside scene.

Deliberately she was not wearing her watch and so she ate her sandwiches when hunger made her stomach rumble. Her seat and table were sun-warmed rocks and, throwing a crust to the seagulls, she sighed with contentment.

It was the sound of breaking waves which brought her sharply back to reality. The tide was swirling only a few metres away and looking back the way she had come, she gasped in dismay. The tide had nearly engulfed the rocks she had scrambled over, waves breaking over them in white sprays.

Panic making her heart hammer, she struggled into her shoes then grabbing her backpack, ran along the cliff base looking for a path. But there wasn't one. Frightened, she ran to the sea's edge. Should she try to swim for it? But seeing the way the white-crested waves were beginning to swirl amongst the rocks, she knew she wouldn't stand a chance.

In movies, stranded girls screamed for help, but Ella's throat was tight with fear, mouth dry. But anyway, who would hear her above the noise of waves and screeching seagulls?

She had never known a tide come in so rapidly, forcing her back until she was only a few metres from the cliff base, a difference in colour showing clearly the high tide line well above her head.

'Ella! Ella!'

The wind distorted her name, but she heard enough to look around in a mixture of hope and bewilderment. Then she saw Will scrambling, slipping over the rocks.

When a wave broke near him, spray momentarily obscuring him, she ran towards him. 'Will, I'm here! I'm here!'

'Come on!' he shouted. 'The tide's coming in fast. You'll get wet, but go to where the rocks are flatter, that way you'll be quicker.'

Oliver as usual excited by the crashing waves, ran splashing and barking between Will and Ella. Perhaps it was the dog's exuberance which made Will slip. Hearing his sharp exclamation, Ella paused to glance towards him, gasping with alarm when she saw he appeared to be wedged between two rocks.

Now it was her turn to call out reassuring as she scrambled, slid on wet seaweed, sometimes slipping into deep pools.

'Ella, I'm OK. You take care. I'm . . . just . . . going . . . to try to lift myself free.'

'I'm coming!' she shouted back. 'Hang on!'

Worried by Will's obvious inability to free himself, her speed was reckless as she hurried to reach him. If the shortest way was to wade in a pool then she did so. She had to free Will before the tide came in completely.

When she reached him, he had managed to haul himself nearly out of the narrow gap. But the swirling sea was now level with the top of the rocks, making it difficult for him to see handholds.

'Will, what can I do? Give me your arm and I'll pull you.'

'You're not strong enough,' he gasped. 'Look, can you take my hand, guide it to somewhere firm so I've something to pull against?'

She was so wet with sea water that she didn't realise she was crying until Will ordered her brusquely to stop. 'Crying won't help! We both need to keep calm.'

But although it took a lot to make Ella cry, once she had started, she couldn't switch off tears like a tap. So instead she bit her lip, holding her breath when a sob threatened to escape. Finding a crevice in which he could slide in the fingers of his left hand, she held his wrist. She might not be able to haul him out, but holding him might stop him falling back.

'Come on, Will!' she urged. 'One . . . two . . .' She didn't manage to say 'three' for a rasping sob stopped it.

Then with a grunt of effort, Will hauled himself on to the rock beside her. Kneeling, he turned his hand so he was holding hers. Then releasing it, he urged, 'Thanks! But come on, we've got to hurry. Keep close to me.'

When a swirling gully of sea stopped them, Will paused, assessing whether he could jump across and if Ella would be able to follow. Seeing him bend his knees slightly, Ella closed her eyes. If he fell . . .

'Ella, jump!' he ordered. 'Just one last effort and we'll be safe.'

'I don't think . . .'

'Jump!' he ordered. 'Look, I'll catch you.'

Seeing him hold out his left arm, she jumped, but being shorter, not so strong, she teetered on the rock's edge.

'I've got you.' His arm was right around her, clamping her to his chest. For a moment which seemed like eternity, they were so close she could feel his breath fanning her face, his lips so near . . .

'I know this isn't the time or place . . .' He kissed her with such force she would have fallen if he hadn't held her so tightly. But it was so swift she hadn't time to respond, react.

'Sorry. I shouldn't have done that. Come

on.' Holding hands, they splashed and waded the last few yards to the shingle in front of Watch Cottage.

'Oliver? Where's Oliver?' Releasing Ella, and whistling, Will ran to the higher ground by the cottage. 'I can't see him anywhere. Ella, can you remember the last time you saw him? Perhaps he's gone home . . .'

As Will began running towards the cliff steps, Ella scrabbled in her backpack for her car keys. 'Will, wait! You'll be quicker and safer in the car.'

As though sensing the urgency, the car started immediately, seeming to race up the steep road. Will was out of the car before Ella brought it to a halt, but hearing his shout of delight and Oliver barking, she was suddenly overwhelmed by emotion. Her hands still gripping the steering wheel, her head dropped down on them. Sobbing, she didn't hear Will returning.

'There! There now. It's all right!' Opening her door, he leaned in to gently lift her face, turning it towards him.

His lips were only inches away as he said huskily, 'Come on, we both need to dry out and have a warm drink. And we've some unfinished business . . .'

CHAPTER NINE

Going into the kitchen, Will steered Ella into the chair near the Aga, and gently taking her arm, lowered her into it. She tried to say she was sorry, but couldn't.

'Come on. Take deep breaths . . . That's better. Now we both need dry clothes.'

Dry clothes? Hers were at Watch Cottage. 'I'd better go . . .'

'You're not going anywhere!' Will hurried from the room returning quickly with clothes draped over his arm. 'Here, take these,' he ordered. 'The bathroom is the second door on the right. Have a hot shower then put these on.'

'Aren't those Linzi's?' she asked. From the smart cut of the denims and the expensive top, she knew they must belong to the flamboyant magenta-haired girl.

'I can assure you they're not mine! Now, go and do as I say.'

'They'll be too small. I'm much bigger than Linzi.'

'Put . . . them . . . on!' He spoke firmly as though to a disobedient child.

Taking them reluctantly, she went to the bathroom and standing under the shower she sighed with enjoyment. It was good to feel hot water, not cold. To be safe.

To her surprise, she found Linzi's clothes fitted her perfectly, except the jeans were a couple of inches too short. She didn't know why, but feeling shy when she opened the bathroom door, she avoided looking at Will.

'I said they'd fit you. Now put the kettle on while I . . .'

His sentence cut short by the closing of the bathroom door, she stood feeling a little dazed. Was she dreaming? The last ten minutes or so had all been so . . . so . . . homely.

It was Oliver sitting in front of her, head on one side, which brought her back to reality.

'I guess you're hungry. Show me where your food is then.'

Finding it was easy, he sat in front of the right cupboard, tail beating a tattoo. The dog eating, Ella looked around the kitchen. She could see the kettle but where was the teapot, the tea? She hesitated.

Will was so untidy, if she opened a cupboard, might things cascade out? Telling herself not to be so silly, she looked carefully until she found what she wanted. Will didn't take as long showering and so by the time the tea was brewed, he was coming into the kitchen, struggling to do up shirt buttons.

She wanted to help but two things held her back. Will's reluctance to accept help . . . and . . . buttoning his shirt seemed somehow dangerous in the unexpected atmosphere of intimacy.

'How do you manage in the shower with the plaster?' she rushed out.

'A very large plastic bag over it. Now, while we drink the tea, soup can be heating on the Aga. In the fridge you'll find a large container of home-made soup, Sal's best.'

As they drank the warming tea, they got out soup bowls and spoons, bread and butter, only talking when necessary. It wasn't uncomfortable, more companionable. When Will cleared just enough space on the table for them to eat, Ella felt he was paying her a compliment. This was how he ate. He wasn't thinking of her as a visitor expecting special attention, polite conversation. But would he remember he'd said they had unfinished business?

The soup finished, he still had said nothing more than light-hearted comments.

'I haven't thanked you properly,' Ella said, getting up to put the soup bowls by the sink. 'I was really frightened. Panicking . . . If you hadn't come . . . "

'Life has an odd way of putting people in the right place at the right time,' he said, following her with the plates.

'You were certainly that!'

'But I can't take credit for knowing where you were. That was Oliver. When you weren't at Watch Cottage, I thought you had gone for a walk. It was Oliver who ran barking to the rocks.'

'Then I'll have to buy him a very large bone the next time I'm in Clifford.'

'And what will you get me?'

Glancing at him, Ella saw his softly spoken question was emphasised by a raised eyebrow. And there was something in his blue eyes which sent a shiver of delicious anticipation down her spine.

His lips brushed hers lightly as though seeking permission. Then feeling her relax, he used his left arm to pull her closer, his urgency underlined by his demanding mouth. She had never felt so caught up in such a whirl of longing, passion. Then suddenly he released her with a deep sigh.

'I'm sorry. I shouldn't have done that.'

She was just going to ask if his 'unfinished business' was the kiss, when moving away, he said, 'I came down to see you about a business proposition.'

She froze. She had got it so very wrong!

'I was wondering if you'd help me sort out my office?' He nodded towards the room linked to The Studio by the archway. 'I'll pay you of course.'

Stunned, she could only look at him dumbly.

'I'm sorry! I thought you might be glad of some work. Audrey said she couldn't pay you much and I need help. But I quite understand if after, if after . . .'

As Ella took a deep breath, she

unexpectedly felt in control of the situation. They had kissed. So what? It had been a silly romantic gesture, that was all. She needed money, he needed help.

'Of course I'll help. What is it you want me to do?'

'Have you time to go to the office for me to show you?'

Will's eagerness had Ella taking a deep breath. He certainly was keen to erase any memory of that kiss.

Going through the archway into the small office and seeing the piles of bills, invoices, shade cards, swatches of material, Ella's urge to be tidy, businesslike, took over.

'Sorry about the mess,' he apologised. 'I'm not normally like this. With the cottage way behind schedule I seem to have lost the ability to think, do things in the right order.'

'You don't have to explain. When do you want me to start?'

'Start what?' Linzi's sharp question made them both turn, startled. 'I didn't hear the car,' Will said, moving away from Ella.

'I've had a puncture. The rescue service said they'd be ages, so I thought I'd walk here.' Then glaring at Ella, Linzi demanded, 'What are you doing in my clothes? What exactly has been going on?'

'I got caught by the tide. Will rescued me . . .'

'How very romantic! But why didn't you go

to Watch Cottage to get changed?' The question was sharp with suspicion.

'We'd lost Oliver and came here to see if he'd returned,' Will explained. 'And as for your clothes. I don't think you'd mind. Ella was soaked.'

'Well I do mind. Those are very expensive designer labels.'

There was something in Linzi's tone which had Ella retorting, 'I might not be able to afford, "designer labels", but I'm careful with clothes, mine or those belonging to others.'

'So you make a habit of needing a change of clothes, do you?'

'Stop it, both of you! Linzi, I'm sure Ella will take care of your things. And although it's really none of your business, Ella is going to help me sort out the office.'

'I'm supposed to do the paperwork!' Linzi flared.

'Supposed, is right,' Will replied calmly. 'You're not exactly cut out for office work are you?'

Going up to Will and smiling disarmingly, Linzi put her arms around his neck.

'I'd better go,' Ella muttered. 'I'll return your clothes as soon as I've washed . . .'

'No! You'll ruin them. Just bring them back, though I doubt I'll wear them again.'

'Will, I'll see you on Monday.' Ella was surprised by her outward calmness for Linzi's remarks had her longing to retaliate. But that would be to sink to her level.

Ella was relieved that until late on Sunday afternoon she saw no-one for she needed to be alone.

She didn't want to remember the fright of being cut off by the tide, but she kept replaying the feel of Will's kiss, the effect it had on her.

She was sitting on the window seat in her bedroom when Joel drove down so quietly she was unaware of him until he called up to her.

'Hi there, princess. If you're looking for a prince to rescue you, I'm here!'

His comments coupled with his elaborate gestures of trying to climb the drainpipe lifted her spirits dramatically. Running downstairs, she threw open the door with a welcoming smile.

'My goodness is this a case of absence making the heart growing fonder? Not that I'm complaining. Actually I'm glad you're in. I want to repay your hospitality by taking you for a meal. It had better be this evening. I've been staying with friends so I'm freshly showered and dressed respectably.'

Glancing as his well-fitting black chinos and shirt, Ella replied that she doubted she could match his smartness.

'You Ella, would look good in a bin liner. I'm not often wrong in judging people, but I'd say you were oblivious of your stunning bone structure, the very attractive, reassuring openness about you. You've never tried to disguise it when I've riled you. I like that. I know where I am with you. One day perhaps . . .'

But when Linzi's car sent seagulls wheeling noisily into the sky, Joel touched Ella's face fleetingly. 'About seven?'

Ella was just closing the door when she heard Linzi's deliberately loud voice. 'Hi Joel. Don't say that little frump has bewitched you too!'

Ella did not hear Joel's reply, but she did hear when Linzi shouted to her,

'And don't you go closing the door on me. I've a lot to say to you.' Remaining outside, Ella did shut the door.

She did not want that angry girl in Watch Cottage, shattering its peace. 'And you can go,' Linzi ordered Joel. 'This is between her and me.'

'Ella does have a name,' he reminded, not moving.

'Joel, please do as Linzi says. This really has nothing to do with you.'

Shrugging, he walked towards his tent and when she gauged he was out of earshot, Linzi spoke quietly but with an edge of menace which chilled Ella.

'I'm warning you, keep away from Will. Pretending to be cut off by the tide so he rescues you is an old trick!'

'I wasn't pretending. And for your information, it was Oliver who alerted him.'

'You've even managed to get that dog to like you!'

Ella's slight smile at such a silly comment infuriated Linzi even more.

'You come here playing the Miss innocent, butter wouldn't melt in your mouth . . .'

As Linzi raised her voice, Joel came striding back.

'Linzi, that's enough!' he ordered. 'Why are you making such a scene? Anyone would think you loved Will.' Then narrowing his eyes, he questioned quietly, 'You haven't fallen for him, have you?'

It was now Joel's turn to feel Linzi's full fury. 'It's none of your business.'

'But it is very much my business, or I thought it was.'

On the sidelines now, Ella saw the flash of something passing between him and Linzi.

'Oh go and play your silly little games,' Linzi threw at Ella.

Getting back into the banana-yellow car, Linzi roared back up the hill, Ella and Joel stood in silence, both listening for the same thing, but for different reasons.

'She didn't go back to Will then,' Joel smiled, as the fading sound of the sports car indicated Linzi was heading towards Clifford. 'Now where were we? Ah yes, you were going to get ready for me to take you out. Can I wait inside?'

As Ella turned to open the door, she was

73

stopped by Joel's next question. 'By the way, have you fallen for Will?'

'To echo Linzi, it's none of your business. Now, are we going out, or not?'

'Yes, we most certainly are and to a very special place.'

As Ella ran up the stairs to change, she thought Joel's generosity was his way of making up for the scene with Linzi. She didn't see his cold, tight-lipped smile.

CHAPTER TEN

Ella had left most of her 'town' clothes with a friend, but she had brought her favourite dress with her. Mid-calf length, the silk clung to her body, the skirt's soft folds drifting as she moved.

A light knock on the front door had Ella quickly misting on a delicate perfume, then picking up her small black suede handbag, she walked carefully down the stairs. But opening the door, her confidence evaporated. Joel would be used to sophisticated beauties like Linzi . . .

'Wow! Ella, you look . . .' Joel paused, searching for the right word. 'Lovely' was too trite . . . 'Stunning' was too . . . too . . . Then he smiled. 'Ella, goddess of moonlight! You don't know how apt that is,' he said. Ella felt a tingle

74

of excitement. What was it about men in black that made her go weak at the knees?

'Are you all right?' he asked, turning to give her his arm.

She nodded. She dare not risk speaking in case her voice was tight, squeaky with embarrassment at her thoughts!

They didn't speak again until Joel drew up outside a low, rambling old house. A discreet board with gold letters on holly green proclaimed, *Art and Eat in the Country.*

Helping her down from the vehicle, Joel took her hand as he led her to the open door. Ella was surprised that instead of a conventional hall, it was more like a sitting-room. But many of the comfortable chairs and sofas were facing walls hung with skilfully lit pictures.

'Ah Joel, we have the privilege of seeing you again and with your usual luck you've managed to charm yet another . . .'

'Ella,' Joel interrupted hastily. 'This is Marcus, the owner.'

As the middle-aged man took her hand, muttering banal pleasantries, she looked around puzzled. The house, the comfortable room, didn't look at all like an art gallery.

'Are we too late for a table?' Joel asked Marcus.

'You know I always keep one tucked away for special guests.' Then turning to Ella, he added, 'And you can't get more special than

Joel, can you?'

Not knowing what he was talking about, Ella hoped a vague smile would belie her confusion. Then Marcus opened wide double oak doors into a dining room where ten or so tables were already occupied by diners. But to her discomfort, they were being escorted to the farthest side of the room and as they passed tables, people glanced up at first casually, but then seeing Joel, smiled.

Some congratulated him, trying to detain him with a hand on his arm, but it was obvious from the clever way he extricated himself with a charming smile and a couple of words, that he was used to this.

Reaching a table for two tucked in an alcove which although a good distance from the others, was plainly visible, Joel's smile faded as he muttered to Marcus, 'Why on earth do you keep your reserve table in such a prominent place?'

'Business. Joel, you of all people should recognise the need for that.' Marcus was pulling out a chair for Ella so she couldn't see his face, but she heard the hardness of his tone.

Conscious of several people looking and obviously talking about them, Ella wished she could close her eyes and find herself back in Watch Cottage. She wasn't aware she had slouched in her chair, trying to make herself as small as possible until she heard Marcus

76

comment softly to Joel that she wasn't at all like 'the other one who enjoyed being looked at.'

Annoyed at being compared unfavourably with the mysterious 'other one', Ella sat up straighter. But this more purposeful posture did not prevent Joel ordering from the menu for her.

As Marcus left, Joel leaned across to whisper, 'Ella, do try to look as though you're enjoying yourself.'

'How can I when you order for me and it's obvious this is not a normal restaurant and you're some sort of celebrity? You should have warned me.'

'Then you wouldn't have come,' he said flatly. 'I thought you needed a break and being a normal red-blooded male, I like being in the company of pretty girls.'

'You've a harem?' she asked. Aware one or two diners were still watching them, she smiled as she spoke, but her tone was icy. 'I suppose the "other one" is some glamorous blonde but this particular evening, I was all you could find.'

'Oh Ella, for goodness' sake don't be so prickly. And if it makes you relax, Marcus was referring to Linzi. Why can't you believe that I asked you just because I thought you needed a change from Will and that dog of his.' Then seeing a waiter coming towards them, he reached across to take her hand. 'At least enjoy the food. It really is excellent.'

Moving a vase of lemon daffodils so she was partially hidden from curious eyes, Ella did indeed enjoy the meal and the champagne Marcus insisted she had. But Joel drank sparkling Malvern water, explaining he had no wish to kill himself or others and it was vital he had a driving licence to enable him to get about the country.

He was so unusually serious, that caught off guard, Ella laughingly remarked he could always change careers like Will had done. But at the mention of Will's name, Joel's laugh was a sarcastic preface to, 'You'd think an architect-cum-builder wouldn't have fallen off a ladder, wouldn't you? Especially when he was only about a metre off the ground. But perhaps he hasn't a head for heights which is why he took to doing up cottages. I ask you, what challenge is that for a man?'

'Does life have to be a "challenge"?' Ella asked, thoughtfully stirring her black coffee. 'I think doing up cottages for people to use for holidays is really worthwhile.'

'A week or two in one of those dumps will soon be forgotten. But my landscapes will always be there for people to admire, to enjoy.'

But before Ella could reply, a large woman in flowing purple descended on them. Bending over Joel she was embarrassingly coy as she gushed, 'I hope you'll excuse me interrupting you two love birds, but I just had to come and say how much I admire your work. I've just bought the very big one of Scotland. It's just the thing for my drawing room. I'm going to try to capture the essence of the Highlands in the décor. Misty purple I think . . .'

Although Joel seemed to be smiling, his eyes were cold as he corrected, 'Not Scotland, Snowdonia. I hope it will still be "just the thing" for your drawing room. And as it was in Wales, will your décor consist of red dragons?'

Ella cringed inwardly at Joel's heavy tone, but the woman either didn't hear, or chose to ignore it. 'Not only a true artist, but witty too. I must . . .'

'Go back to your table,' Joel finished. 'I'm sure you're anxious to discuss your changed decorating plans.'

Standing up abruptly, he nearly sent the woman staggering, but catching hold of her arm, he steadied her. Bending, he whispered something in her ear which had her colouring slightly. The look she sent him over her shoulder as she left, had Ella wondering what on earth he could have said.

But when she asked him, he replied, 'Come on, let's go into the gallery before anyone else collars me. If you're to succeed, you have to learn very quickly the way of getting around people. Sometimes it's a smile, sometimes a silly compliment, or joining in when they begin to hold forth on the "hidden meaning" in my work. And to be honest my looks help too. If I looked like the back of a bus I'd have a much harder time.'

In the gallery, Joel steered her towards a seascape framed in bleached wood, Ella held back a little, startled by his honesty about his looks. Or was it vanity? But he appeared not to notice when he asked her what she thought of the photograph. He seemed so genuine that after a minute or two's contemplation she was lost in the beauty of a tranquil lake.

'You like it?' he asked eventually.

When she nodded, he took her hand to lead her to where smaller pictures were attractively displayed.

'Come and look at this one,' he said eagerly. 'I think you'll see why the colour of your frock was so right.'

The picture might have been smaller than many of the others, but its size added an intimacy. The light of a full moon reflected on sand and was so magical that Ella gasped.

'It's, it's . . . I don't know what to say.'

When he took it off the wall and handed it to her, she looked in amazement first at the picture then at him.

'It's yours. I know you really like it for what it shows, not that it matches some horrible wallpaper, or your frock! If that dreadful woman or one like her, should buy it . . .'

'Thank you,' she said formally. Sometimes a kiss was added to the thanks, but she held back from kissing this particular man, even though in such a public place with others around, it would have been just a peck on the cheek.

As he led her around the other pictures, she held his gift close to her. Passing a price list, her eyes were drawn almost magnetically to the large amount being asked for her moonlight picture.

'Joel,' she gasped. 'I can't possibly take this. It's far too expensive . . . I hardly know you . . .'

She had her back to the entrance and so did not see Will come in with Linzi. But Joel had. 'To you, my price is a kiss,' he smiled, pointing to his cheek. 'Please Ella, humour me.'

Although her high heels meant she was at the right level to kiss his cheek, he bent towards her. At the last moment, he turned his face sharply so her lips met his. She tried to recoil but he held her firmly. That she was not returning his kiss, did not seem to bother him.

But it bothered two onlookers. Will and Linzi. After the first shock of seeing Ella kissing Joel in such a public place, Will noticed her rigid back, one hand clenched by her side. A few rapid strides had him ordering, 'Joel, leave her alone!'

Will might only have had one good hand, but he used it to good effect, spinning Joel away from Ella.

'Been hitting the bottle too much,' Joel drawled loudly. 'You really should watch it. Attacking people can land you in serious trouble.'

Nearly blinded by tears of embarrassment and shame, Ella ran to the door, barging into Linzi. 'What do you think you're playing at?' she whispered venomously, seizing Ella's arm. But she had taken care to have her back to the room so to avid onlookers she appeared to be comforting. 'How can a plain Jane like you have two men quarrelling over you?'

Wrenching herself free, Ella hurried outside, but Linzi followed. 'You'll not win. I can have whichever of those two I want, at any time. Your feeble designs are pathetic!'

'You're welcome to them!' Ella retorted. But although she spoke with quiet contempt, she wanted to run, to get as far away as possible from the three people who seemed to thrive on scenes.

Never had she been caught up in such a drama. And she didn't really understand how it had happened. She had no 'designs' on either Joel or Will.

She walked rapidly across to the car park entrance, shoulders straight, head held high. As far as she was concerned Linzi, Joel and Will could play their little games without her,

Watching, Linzi smiled. It was a long walk back to Watch Cottage, especially in high heels.

CHAPTER ELEVEN

It wasn't long before Ella realised her shoes were not fit for country roads and so slipping them off, she carried them with the photograph Joel had given her.

Walking carefully on the grass verge, she knew that as the road only led to the bay and Peace Farm, no car would come along and stop. Although there was just enough moon and star light for her to see, the bright sweep of a car's headlights caught her by surprise. When it stopped with a splutter of grit, Ella tried to merge into the hedge. If she stood very still . . .

'Ella? What on earth are you doing?' Sal was running back to her.

'It's too complicated to explain.'

'I knew something like this would happen.' Gently taking Ella's arm, Sal asked, 'How about a cup of tea at the farm?'

Sal's kindness after such a dreadful scene made Ella sag slightly. Sal said nothing as she led Ella back to the farm vehicle, where she hastily pushed odds and ends off the passenger seat.

It was when they were cradling mugs of tea in the farmhouse kitchen that Sal asked almost casually. 'Want to tell me what happened?'

Ella hesitated, then the homeliness of the

untidy kitchen, the old dog sleeping on the hearth mat, precipitated a tangled outpouring. Sal had to question gently before she fully understood.

'That Linzi . . . She's trouble. I've told Will, but he won't listen. I never would have thought he would make such a scene in public.' Then, seeing how Ella was slumped in her chair, Sal offered, 'How about staying here the night?'

'No thank you. You're very kind. But I'd like to get back to Watch Cottage.'

* * *

Her dress thrown carelessly on the bed, Ella sat on the window seat of her tower bedroom, the cotton of her nightshirt cool against her skin. Looking out, she frowned at the darkness of the night. It was as though the heavy cloud was matching her mood.

She wanted to try to sort out what had happened, but a part of her shied away from it. What if Will, Joel and Linzi had now completely destroyed what she had hoped to find at Watch Cottage? Had she inadvertently become enmeshed in a love triangle?

Ella didn't know when she had fallen asleep, but when coldness woke her, she guessed it must have been a few hours. But although the cosiness of the duvet seemed a quick solution, she hurriedly dressed in warm clothes.

Going down the narrow stairs a sudden

feeling of being shut in, trapped, had her going to the front door. Throwing it open, she gulped in the cold night air. Eyes shut, she concentrated on calming down. When her heartbeat had slowed down, she took a few steps into the still, starry night.

It was then she saw the faint outline of Joel's vehicle. Running back into the cottage, she closed the door, then leaned against it. When had he returned? It must have been when she was asleep. Going to a window, she cautiously peered out. She didn't realise she was holding her breath until seeing no sign of any movement, a long sigh escaped. But this was quickly swamped by a feeling of alarm.

Suppose he was sitting in the car watching the cottage? She should have stayed with Sal! Should she phone her? But what could she say? Joel really wasn't doing anything. But, however firmly she kept repeating this and knowing it was true, she felt trapped.

Grabbing her car keys, Ella ran out, not bothering to lock the door. She knew the engine might wake Joel but if just for once, the car started first time . . . Driving up the hill, the car's noise seemed so loud that she cowered back in her seat as though this would lessen it. Repeatedly she glanced in the rear-view mirror for following headlights. Joel must have heard her. In his powerful vehicle he would soon catch up.

She had no idea where she was going,

except she had to get away. A rabbit running across the road made her brake and it was then she saw the narrow lane leading off on her right.

Turning, she drove slowly, teeth gritted as she peered through the windscreen. She mustn't go into a ditch. But as her headlights bounced on to a high hedge, she realised she was in the lane where Will had his cottage!

Stopping, she bit her lip. What should she do? Joel had found it difficult to turn in the narrow lane and in broad daylight. She would just have to wait until there was enough daylight for her to see properly.

But after a few minutes, restlessness had her searching for the torch she kept in the car for emergencies. She would go for a walk. See where the lane led. At first the rustles and noise of the night made her stop, looking around anxiously. Then seeing another rabbit, she smiled at her silliness.

The sudden sound of a powerful vehicle on the road made her hastily switch off her torch. Although she was holding her breath, she couldn't still the hammering of her heart. Was Joel looking for her? Stumbling into ruts she ran in panic. Her car was blocking the lane, so if he did come, he would be on foot.

Why, oh why, had she left the security of Watch Cottage? Out in the open she was so vulnerable. It was then she saw a gap in the tall hedge, a small gate askew on broken hinges.

There was just enough room for her to squeeze through . . .

All silent again, she switched on the torch and carefully swinging its beam in an arc, she saw a two up, two down, dilapidated house. Surrounded by bushes and a few small trees, a few lower branches were broken as though an animal habitually went that way. As Ella cautiously moved forward, she smiled. Here she was, looking for broken or bent branches like a child playing at stalking a wild animal!

The rough path led around the house, but Ella stopped at the front door. Pushing it gently, she sighed with relief as it creaked open enough for her to enter. A sweep of her torch showed a room with peeling wallpaper, tattered curtains hanging on a broken rail. But it was an upturned chair which caught her attention.

It was only then she realised how exhausted she was. Turning the chair the right way up, she moved it to the window, placing it carefully so the curtains hid her if anyone should look into the house.

She relaxed as she realised that even if the vehicle she'd heard had been Joel's, he hadn't come down the lane . . . But what on earth had made her think he would have come looking for her?

But Ella didn't get any further for her head fell forward in exhausted sleep.

It was Oliver's wet nose thrust into her hand

which wide her with a cry of fright. Alarmed she looked down at him, then around her. Where was she? How had she got here?

'Ella! It's me, Sal. You OK?' she asked, coming in and crouching down in front of her.

She rubbed her eyes to banish sleep but also to try to clear her mind. 'What are you doing here? And Oliver?'

'We came looking for you. We were worried.'

Hopefully Sal paused, waiting for Ella to explain, but when she seemed intent on stroking Oliver, Sal asked gently, 'Did something happen at Watch Cottage to frighten you? Joel . . .'

'No, he didn't do anything. I just . . . I had to get away.'

'You should have stayed with me. It's not turning out to be as peaceful here as you had hoped, is it?'

'I love Watch Cottage and you've been so kind . . .'

'But not to me.' Will was standing just outside the front door where he could hear, but not be seen. 'Ella, can I come in?'

When she saw Ella's indecision, Sal soothed, 'You don't have to see Will. But he is very worried about you. It was hardly light when he went down to see if you were all right. Then seeing Joel gone and your door unlocked, he phoned me.

'Earlier, when I heard a car in this lane, I

got up to look and seeing a flash of torchlight, thought it was just lads out after rabbits. It was Oliver who led us here. He's a good dog is that one. Should be in the police.'

'Ella?' Will's soft question reminded he was waiting for her reply.

As she told Will he could come in, Sal patted her hand reassuringly. Straightening up in the chair, Ella kept her eyes averted as Will entered. He stopped a couple of metres from her. That she had come to this place, in the middle of the night, must indicate her deep unhappiness. Frightened even.

'Ella, can Sal go now? She really does have things to do at the farm.'

'Of course, and Sal, thanks for everything. I'm sorry I've been such a nuisance.'

Kissing Ella lightly on the cheek, Sal whispered, 'Don't act too hastily. I made that mistake.'

Neither Ella nor Will moved or spoke until they heard Sal drive away. Then holding out his hand, Will asked softly, 'Ella, will you come to the cottage I'm doing up? At least that's clean. This dilapidated house is no place to try to sort things out.'

When she hesitated, he moved slowly to her, hand still outstretched. This time Ella took it and was glad of the firmness of his hold, she stood up a little unsteadily.

*   *   *

With Oliver running ahead, they went in silence to Green Cottage. It would, Ella thought, have been romantic, the hand holding, Will's obvious concern, except for her chaotic thoughts.

Taking the key from under an upturned flower pot, Will opened the door, standing aside for Ella to enter, he ordered Oliver to stay outside. Going into the kitchen, he returned awkwardly carrying a folding chair.

'Let me help.' As Ella took it, Will nodded his thanks before fetching another one.

'Where shall we sit?' he asked.

'I like this room,' Ella said, looking around. 'I've peeped in through the windows when Oliver led me here the day I brought him to the farm.'

Although there wasn't a fire in the small grate, they sat either side of it. The space between them seemed natural, not too close, nor so far apart that it gave the feeling of hostility.

Seeing her tightly clasped hands in her lap, he sensed she didn't know how to begin, how to tell him what had made her leave Watch Cottage in the night.

So hoping he wouldn't make matters worse, he said quietly, 'Ella, I'm truly sorry about last night. I shouldn't have acted as I did. I thought Joel was up to his usual tricks. But perhaps you don't find his kiss . . .?' Leaving his question unfinished, he put his head questioningly on one side.

As though to reinforce her answer, Ella met his questioning gaze. 'I didn't want him to kiss me, if that's what you mean. And he hasn't done so before.'

'I was surprised to see you there with him after we'd half arranged to go. You offered to drive . . .'

'You were there with Linzi!'

'She insisted.' He paused, before adding slowly, 'I think she knew you would be there with Joel, wanted me to see you with him.'

'I can't think why. I hardly know him.'

'I've known Linzi since she was small girl and she's always been the jealous type.'

'Are you saying she was jealous of me being with Joel?'

Will shrugged. 'Who knows. But she tends to be a control freak. After this,' he said, indicating his plastered arm. 'She certainly tries to organise me, my business.' Then leaning forward he asked, 'Do you want to tell me why you left Watch Cottage?'

'I felt suddenly so overwhelmed.' She spoke slowly as though thinking about every word. 'I'm not used to scenes like that. My life has been comparatively dull. I'm the sort who doesn't like to stand out, have people stare at me.'

'Oh dear, and that's just what I made happen. And I thought I was rescuing you!'

'You were in a way,' she admitted. 'I'd felt slightly out of my depth all evening, I didn't know Joel was quite so . . . famous. And then Linzi said . . .'

'Said what?'

'I guess she was jealous just as you said. But she has no reason to be. I thought Joel was just asking me out for a meal just out of kindness.'

'Perhaps he was, to begin with, until he saw me come in with Linzi.'

'You think he deliberately kissed me to make Linzi jealous?' Ella asked incredulously. 'But why?'

'Perhaps it wasn't for Linzi's benefit, but for . . .'

But Will didn't finish for Oliver came bounding in. Going over to Ella, he put a beseeching paw on her lap.

Although they smiled, Ella and Will both sighed inwardly. Will, that he hadn't finished what he was going to say. Ella, wondering how he would have finished the sentence.

CHAPTER TWELVE

'I'm going to Watch Cottage with you!' Ella had drawn up by Will's gate, but instead of him getting out, he said firmly, 'There's no way you're going there by yourself.'

Although he had turned in his seat to look

at her, Ella stared straight ahead as she kept the engine ticking over. 'You think Joel might say or do, something?' she asked.

'He's not one to let go of something when he's got his teeth into it.'

'Meaning me?'

She was still not looking at him and as her voice was flat, neutral, Will couldn't gauge her reaction. 'No, of course not! I meant . . . Look, Ella, believe me, it's nothing directly to do with you.'

'But indirectly?' she questioned, remembering what Joel had said about Will always being good at everything. Having chances in life . . . But how did she fit into whatever was going on between the two men?

When Will did not reply, she said, 'I think I understand Joel just a little.'

'You might think so, but he's very manipulative.'

'Aren't we all, one way or another?' She slanted him a cool, enquiring glance.

'Exactly how have I "manipulated" you?' Will asked icily.

'Aren't you doing that now? Insisting you'll come down with me?'

'That's concern! If you don't know the difference, then perhaps you should think about it.'

He got out of the car so quickly that it rocked and when his plastered arm hit the door, he swore under his breath. Opening the back door, he ordered Oliver to get out. Then slamming that door shut, Will was just about to do the same to the passenger door when he paused. Bending down, his eyes as cold as polar seas, sent a shiver down Ella's spine.

His voice was equally cold as he said, 'Although today is when you're supposed to start working for me, it would be better all round if we cancelled the arrangement.'

She winced as he slammed the door, but thrusting the car into gear, she drove down the hill at a pace which was far from safe. She was so angry that at first she didn't notice Joel had gone. His tent, the few things he had scattered around it, all gone. The only reminder, a patch of flattened yellowish turf. Getting out of the car, she ran to the sea's edge and with her back to it, scanned the small bay. Yes, he really had gone!

For the rest of that day, Ella half wondered if Will would phone to apologise, asking her if she would be prepared to work for him, help him. But the phone was silent, except for a call from Sal, asking if she was all right. Although Ella did not want to talk in case she gave something away, she did chat cautiously for a few minutes, before making a vague excuse.

Presumably Linzi had long gone and with Will silent, Ella realised there was only one other person who could upset the quietness of the bay. Joel. She might not be able to stop him if he came back and camped outside

Watch Cottage but she would keep her distance. She rehearsed, 'if he said that', then she would reply . . . But what would she reply?

The next day, to still her thoughts, to blank out Joel and Will, she kept busy, giving the cottage a spring clean which Audrey never seemed to have done. She also took Oliver for a walk, going cautiously to the back gate of The Studio where he always waited for her. It would be silly, childish, to let the dog suffer because of what had happened.

The cottage spotless, Ella next turned her attention to the bay, gathering up every bit of driftwood and bagging rubbish washed up by the tide. But when the beach was as clean as a picture in a tourist brochure, she stood hands on hips, looking at the pile of rubbish bags.

The bin men never ventured down the steep road to the bay and so she had to take bin bags up to Will's gate on the appropriate day. But she couldn't leave so many bags there, he might see it as provocative.

So loading them into the car, she was halfway up the hill before she realised she had no idea where the recycling depot was. She didn't want to call in at Peace Farm in case Sal began talking to her about Will, Joel and Linzi.

Driving towards Clifford, she saw a man on a bike and hoping he was local, she asked where she could take the bags and was pleased it was near the town.

Afterwards, she would go into a café to

wash her hands before treating herself to a cream cake and coffee.

This change of scene, seeing other people, relaxed Ella so much that she decided to explore the network of small roads and lanes. She was intrigued by the unusual names of the villages, some of which were little more than a handful of houses and cottages.

It was obvious several pubs and small shops had been converted into houses but even the smallest hamlet had a church, most of them surprisingly large, presumably built by landowners wanting to impress their neighbours. But seeing a tiny church built in the middle of a field, Ella stopped. There was no sign of a village and she hadn't passed a house for a mile or more.

Intrigued, she parked the car near a small gate in a low stone wall. This opened on to the field where a path had been mown through the grass to the church. As Ella followed the path, the turreted roof of a large house came into view on the skyline.

Of course, the church must have been built for the owners. Another, more ornate gate led into the little churchyard where moss-bayred gravestones lent at odd angles, sometimes shaded by ancient yew trees.

To Ella's delight, the church door was unlocked and going into the cool interior, she was surprised by its simplicity. Perhaps the people who had built the turreted house had run out of money by the time it came to the church!

Outside again, she realised from the great girth of the yew trees that they were very old. Going over to one standing in a corner by the wall, she looked up into its dark green depths. It was then she heard voices. Should she be there? After all it did look part of an estate. It was a reflex action which made her squeeze between tree and wall, but as the voices came nearer, she wished she had not. Better to be ticked off for trespassing than caught skulking like a naughty child!

She was just going to come out of hiding when she heard a voice she knew. Joel! In panic she sagged down, trying to make herself as small as possible.

'Don't be so impatient!' His reprimand though, was softened by a laugh. 'I'm working. This is the breakthrough I've been wanting, recording the landscape and buildings on large estates. Owners can't afford artists these days, but they can afford me.'

'One day I'm going to live in a big house.'

It was Linzi!

'Not one of Will's twee cottages then?'

'It's fun doing them up. If I can persuade Will to be more adventurous, buy several properties, charge high rents, then he'll end up rolling in money.'

'Princess, I really can't see that happening, Will's much too cautious, he's not got my ambition.'

'Ambition hasn't got you very far, has it?' she remarked sarcastically. 'Travelling around all the time, sometimes living in that tent . . .'

'I don't expect you to understand, but photography is my life, the one thing I've always wanted to do. But one day I shall be a name everyone recognises, whereas Will . . .'

'Oh, I'm tired of you and Will, the silly hang-up you have about him. For goodness' sake let's get into this dreary little church so you can finish. Then we'll find a nice pub . . .'

Ella heard the church door open, and when their voices were cut off by its closing, she climbed over the wall and ran back to her car.

Would she never be rid of them? she fumed, driving back to Watch Cottage as fast as the narrow lanes would allow. Although from what she had heard, Joel had a good reason to be still in the area, why was Linzi still there? Did Will know?

But once she had reached the bay, Ella calmed down. Those three were no concern of hers.

The next day was so warm that Ella took out a chair and sitting against the shelter of the cottage wall, read one of Audrey's books about the area. There were tales of smugglers, hauntings, villages swallowed by the sea during storms, and Watch Cottage was mentioned too.

She was so engrossed she didn't hear Sal's

vehicle until it bumped across the shingle. Closing the book, and seeing who it was, she hurried to meet her, smiling broadly.

But Sal hadn't noticed this. 'Ella, I'm worried about Will,' she began through the open window, even before she had turned off the engine. Then seeing the shadow of worry on Ella's face, she added hastily as she got out, 'Not his health. I took him to have his plaster off yesterday and the hospital seem pleased. Look, can we go inside? I don't want to be overheard!'

Ella looked around quickly, but although the bay was deserted, she led the way indoors. Shutting the door firmly, she asked, 'What is it? If Will's OK I don't see what . . .'

'Let's sit down. I've been up since dawn, then I saw that van . . . It's not local, that's not good enough for the likes of her. It's come from . . .'

'I'm sorry,' Ella interrupted. 'I don't understand.'

'He's a fool and I've told him so to his face.'

'Who? The van driver?'

'No, Will! I've just come from there, but he thinks I'm exaggerating. He said there must have been some mistake, the van driver had lost his way. I told Will straight, if that was so, then the van would soon have turned around. There are no big, smart houses up that lane, so he must have been going to Green Cottage.'

'Sal, I'm sorry, but I still don't see . . .'

'She's bewitched him, that's what she's done.'

Sal said this with such conviction that Ella burst out laughing. 'Will, bewitched? I don't believe it!'

'Then how do you account for the fact that even after I told him what I thought was happening, he as good as told me to mind my own business?'

'It seems he doesn't like to be organised by women,' Ella said ruefully.

'I've been caught like that, too. I thought I was helping . . .'

'Oh dear, so you'll not do any better than me.'

'Do better than you in what way?' Ella asked cautiously as warning bells began ringing. 'What was the van?'

'Decorators.'

'Is that all!'

'No, it isn't. I keep telling you. They're not local. I've seen them in glossy magazines when they do those house makeovers.'

'Perhaps,' Ella said gently. 'That's what Will has got them in to do. It seems reasonable.'

'That's just what it's not! They'll cost a fortune and a fortune is something Will's not got. He sank nearly all his savings into buying that cottage, doing it up himself. He fell off a ladder trying to mend a loose tile. That's how he broke his arm. Of course he tried to carry on, but he's right-handed.'

'But surely Linzi helps when she comes down at weekends?'

'Not her! Have you seen her fingernails? So, if Will won't listen to me . . .'

'No, Sal! I'm not going. If he won't listen to you, then he certainly won't listen to me.'

'He'll be running out of money soon and getting into trouble.'

'What do you mean, "trouble"?'

'He'd got it all planned to the last minute, how long it would take to get the cottage finished, ready for letting this summer. His first bookings for the end of May.'

'The end of May? That's not far away!'

'Come on, Ella, go and talk to him. Make him see sense. If he keeps that fancy firm on, it'll break him financially.'

CHAPTER THIRTEEN

After Sal left, Ella wandered along the beach deep in thought. What should she do about Will? Sal had made it sound as though his plans for the holiday home hung very much in the balance. But if she hadn't been able to get through to him about Linzi's expensive decorators, how could she, Ella?

He hated being organised, so if she tried to talk to him, might she again be accused of doing just that? And what about Linzi? Ella really did not want another confrontation with her, especially as she had a niggle at the back of her mind that Linzi was playing some game with both Will and Joel.

She went to bed still unsure what to do but hoping sleep would bring the answer. To her surprise, she was woken by yells and shrieks of swimmers dashing into the still cold sea. Opening her curtains and seeing a car parked close by the cottage, she saw it was a glorious day.

Four large lads, dressed only in shorts were fooling about, shoving and pushing each other. But what had her frowning was their very loud radio. Dressing hurriedly, Ella went out to ask them politely if they could turn down the radio and perhaps move the car further away. In no mood to be silenced by a girl they vied with each other in passing what they thought were funny comments, but were in fact faintly insulting.

Fuming, Ella stood her ground, but when the one who seemed to be the ringleader asked her if she lived alone, she decided it was time to retreat into the cottage.

She smiled wryly when she found herself wishing Joel was still there. He would soon have sorted them out.

As Ella ate her breakfast she was relieved to hear more people coming down into the bay, but they went to the further end to explore the rocks. It was when the lads began playing football, not bothering if the ball hit the cottage walls, that she decided to go out in the car. But where to? She didn't want to risk bumping into Joel and Linzi.

'What on earth do you think you're doing? Stop kicking that ball against the cottage walls. And turn that radio off!'

These shouted orders, punctuated by Oliver's shrill barking, told Ella that Will was outside and as she thankfully opened the door the dog rushed in. Will though remained outside. Although it was one against four, his stance and manner had the lads moving away, muttering, except for one.

'The radio!' Will reminded sharply. 'Turn it off.'

'What's it to you? You live here or something?'

'What's it to you?' Will echoed him sarcastically. Then he shouted back to the cottage, 'Be a love and put the kettle on! I'm parched after that walk.'

The lad hesitated. The man and dog obviously lived there and although he enjoyed being the big guy with lone girls, a well-muscled man who seemed unperturbed by him and his mates, was another matter. So starting the car, and not bothering to fasten his seat belt, or shut the door, he drove further away with a defiantly roaring engine, the others running after him, shouting for him to stop.

'Ella, can I come in? I'm sorry I shouted to

you about putting on the kettle, but I reasoned that if those oafs thought I was living here, they would move.'

'Yes, of course you can come in. To continue with the realism, I did put it on, though goodness knows why. They would hardly have come in to check, would they?'

As Ella stood by the door, Oliver by her side, she glimpsed an expression on Will's face which puzzled her. It couldn't have been sadness, could it? But then his, 'So, am I welcome after the other day?'

'You mean wanting to see me back here safely and me refusing.' She smiled ruefully. 'We were both a little uptight, weren't we? But if those lads are still watching, hadn't you better come in?'

When Ella indicated a chair by the kitchen table, Will sat down with a sigh.

'It's so hot, do you really want tea?' she asked. 'I've apple juice, spring water or beer.'

'Apple juice would be fine.'

Conscious of him watching as she took the carton from the fridge and poured two glasses, Ella said softly, 'But you did think it your business to warn off those lads. How did you know what was happening? Could you hear the noise?'

'I . . . saw them arrive.'

'Of course, they must have come past your drive.'

When Will seemed to shift uncomfortably,

Ella looked at him searchingly. Could he have been at the end of his garden looking down at the bay and Watch Cottage? But, she told herself firmly, that was silly. There was nothing stopping him looking at the view, after all it was rather special.

'Has Sal been to see you?' Will questioned. He didn't need an answer, Ella's startled apprehension was enough.

'It's OK,' he said, reaching across the table to touch her hand. 'I guessed she would. She's really taken a liking to you. You're the daughter she would have liked to have.'

'She wears a wedding ring, but I haven't seen any sign of a husband,' Ella rushed out. If she could steer the conversation away from what Sal might have said about Will. And it worked.

'Her husband took to the bottle when many dairy farmers found it a hard living. Sal couldn't put up with his drunken behaviour and told him to sober up or go. He went. I think she's regretted it ever since.'

In the ensuing silence, snatches of laughter could be heard from the beach, but no radio. Then Will said apologetically, 'I should have warned you it can get busy here when the weather's good.'

'I don't mind. I can't expect to have this haven all to myself. But you've had the plaster removed. How are your arm and hand?'

'My fingers are OK, but wrist movement is a

little awkward and my arm muscles seem to have gone to nothing. But the physiotherapist has given me exercises which should help.'

'Won't you be going to see her regularly?'

'I really haven't the time, the cottage is way behind as it is.'

'The decorators are in there now, aren't they?'

'No. Sal phoned to say there was no sign of them today. Pity really as then I could have sorted it out.' He paused and when she saw him twirling the empty glass, Ella guessed he was in two minds about something. So, getting up, she went to the cupboard where Audrey kept Oliver's biscuits and gave him a few. Seeing the packet was nearly empty, she wrote dog biscuits on the wall message board.

'He's got you well trained,' Will said absently.

'Will, what's the matter? You seem distracted. Isn't Linzi coming down this weekend?'

'No, she phoned to say she can't come. She also said . . . No, it doesn't matter.'

'If it's about me, then it does matter,' Ella insisted quietly.

'It was nothing really. You know what she's like. She said to tell you Joel wouldn't be here either.'

'Why on earth should she say that? I really don't care where Joel is.'

But then it occurred to her that although

Linzi had said the message was for her, Ella, had Linzi meant it for Will, hinting that she was with Joel? Was she trying to make Will jealous? If so, it hadn't worked, for this possibility didn't seem to have occurred to him.

Then aware Will was looking at her closely, Ella wondered if she had protested too loudly. 'Will, I really don't care where Joel is. If and when he comes back, I'll make sure he understands that as far as I'm concerned, the episode in the gallery is in the past.'

With a nod of what Ella took to be satisfaction, Will got up and going to the door, looked down the length of the bay.

'Those lads seem to have quietened down now, so I'll go. I've a lot to do.'

'Like paperwork?' Ella squirmed inwardly. Had she really said that?

He nodded, then head on one side, he asked, 'Have you forgiven me enough to sort it out?'

When she smiled, he said with delight, 'I'm glad about that. I don't want any bad feeling between us. But I must go to the cottage, see what's happened. Perhaps do a bit.'

'Can you drive yet? I guess you can sort of hold the steering wheel, but you can't steer and change gear with one hand.'

'I'll drive slowly.'

'I would rather you didn't drive at all.' She shut her eyes, waiting for him to say something about organising women, but he didn't. It was the soft touch of Will's hand on her cheek which had her opening her eyes in alarm.

'Sorry, I didn't mean to scare you, but you looked as if you were steeling yourself for something unpleasant. Were you waiting for me to say something about organising women? I know I've rather gone on about that, but my mother organised my father and me, and even as a child, Linzi was bossy.'

'I'm not your mother or Linzi,' Ella said firmly. 'And you know what you said about me not recognising concern? I could say the same about you.'

For a few seconds Will stared down at the floor, then suddenly looking directly at her, he said, 'Thank you, I would like a lift. But could we stop off at The Studio, I've a few things to pick up.'

Will had gone to unlock Green Cottage and Ella was unloading his bag of tools when his loud exclamation of annoyance and incredulity had her running in.

He was standing in the middle of the larger of the two rooms, looking round in disbelief and when Ella saw what the painters had already done, she too was stunned.

'It looks awful. This isn't at all what I wanted,' Will said angrily. 'I wanted plain, gentle colours in keeping with the age of the cottage and its situation. What on earth was Linzi thinking about?'

Standing by him, Ella reminded softly, 'Sal did try to warn you.'

'She makes no secret of the fact that she dislikes Linzi and so I thought she was over-reacting when she saw the name on the van.'

'I think you're doing Sal an injustice. And she's right, the people who've done this aren't ordinary painters and decorators. They're interior designers, experts, and their prices are correspondingly high. Just look at the cans of paint. They've not come from a DIY store.'

'There must have been an army of them here to do so much in a day. It will all have to be changed and goodness knows what they'll charge for that. Linzi knew what I wanted. I'd just bought the paint when I fell off that ladder. The tins are in the kitchen, so why didn't they use them?'

'Perhaps they were told not to.'

'She said I had no imagination, that people would want, expect, something modern, stylish.'

'There are styles and styles. Yours is simple, countrified. Linzi's is . . .'

'Totally wrong!' Then kicking a tin, he worried, 'What on earth am I going to do? The first lot of holidaymakers arrive soon. Apart from the decorating, it needs furnishing.'

'I'll help you.'

'Ella, you're an angel,' Will exclaimed, hugging her.

'Well, well, what have we here?' Ella and

Will did not need to look to know it was Joel.

CHAPTER FOURTEEN

'What are you doing here?' Will demanded as he stared at Joel with undisguised contempt. 'What are you two doing here?' Joel drawled, leaning against the door frame.

'This does belong to me.'

'I would never have thought of using red in a cottage . . . quite daring of you. And what expensive paint! Still, with your luck, you'll soon be raking it in. Or will you?'

'Get out!' Will ordered.

'You, Ella, must like the masterful type. First Will makes a scene over nothing at the gallery and now he's ordering me out . . .'

His face tight with anger, Will went towards Joel, his fist balled in anger. 'Cool down! I'm going. I'm sure Ella doesn't want any more violence.'

Ella and Will stayed quite still until they heard Joel drive away. But her thoughts were like sharp splinters . . . Why had Joel come? Was it to see Linzi's over-the-top colour scheme? Perhaps to then taunt Will?

'Ella!' Will put his arm around her shoulder, 'There's no need to look like a frightened rabbit. I wouldn't have laid a finger on him. I'm not the violent type, unless I see a

110

particular girl being kissed against her will. Also, Joel would like the chance to blacken my name, reputation.'

'But at the gallery . . . He couldn't use that, could he?'

'It was he who was in the wrong, though he could spin it to reflect badly on me.'

'But if he went to the newspapers who like stories like that, I can see the headlines, "Photographer attacked by . . . " Will, it might stop people coming here!'

'He won't do that. I know Marcus well, I supervised the work when he turned the house into a gallery and restaurant. It's Joel's first exhibition and he won't want to upset Marcus so he refuses to exhibit him again and tells other galleries that he's bad news.'

Then Will added softly, 'I'm so sorry, you came here expecting peace and quiet but you must feel you've landed into the middle of a TV soap.'

'I just don't understand . . .'

'Joel thinks I get all the luck and perhaps I do.' He paused, looking at Ella with such intensity that she held her breath. But the moment passed and he continued, 'He'd really enjoy seeing my cottage plans fail.'

'And Linzi? You seem . . . friendly.' Ella looked directly at him. People could tell lies, but often their eyes gave them away.

Will met her gaze steadily. 'I've told you, I've known her for ages. Her father . . .'

'She hints that you're more than just friends,' Ella rushed out throwing caution to the winds.

'That bothers you?'

'No, why should it! I hardly know you.'

'Well perhaps this will help . . .'

His first kiss was swift, but as he drew away and looked into her eyes, he saw there the answer he wanted, to kiss her again. This time their lips met with a certainty that this is what both of them wanted, needed.

Neither of them heard the car, the swift, light footsteps, Oliver's warning growl. 'So Joel was right! You . . . you . . .'

It was on Ella that Linzi vented her jealous rage. Pulling her free from Will's arms, she tried to pummel Ella with clenched fists.

'Linzi, stop that!' Will ordered, pulling her away and clamping her arms by her side. Then he spoke to her soothingly as though she was a child having a tantrum. Ella looked on in amazement. One minute Will had been kissing her with a depth and fervour which had made her feel he really meant it . . . Now he was calming the girl who had attacked her as though she was the only one who mattered.

Suddenly Linzi sagged against Will and when she rested her head against his chest, he continued to talk to her. His voice though, was so low Ella couldn't make out if they were words of endearment or just of comfort.

Then Linzi moved her head slightly to slant

112

Ella a look of such triumph that she ran out of the cottage. Hand clamped over her mouth, she went to the car. But there was no escape. Linzi's car was blocking the lane.

Then remembering the way she had come with Oliver, Ella ran into the fields. She had to get away from Linzi! And Will. What a fool she'd been to be taken in by his lies and kisses. If he came running after her, telling her it was all a mistake . . . But he didn't, the one who did was Oliver.

'Oh you good boy!'

Dropping down on her knees, Ella put her arms around his neck, sobbing into his soft coat. For a few seconds he stood still, then pulled away. Standing up, Ella saw he was running towards Peace Farm. If Sal wasn't to be alarmed by his unexpected appearance, Ella knew she had to follow. Reaching the farmyard, Ella sighed with relief. Thankfully, Sal's vehicle wasn't there.

But what should she do? Had Will and Linzi already returned to The Studio? If not, might they pass her if she walked along the road?

When Oliver looked at her, tail wagging expectantly, she said grimly, 'All right then, back to Watch Cottage.'

Ella didn't realise exactly what she had said until the dog took her along a little-used path across fields, then slithering down a steep path into the bay. She stopped in amazement. The tide was coming fast and it looked to be an

113

unusually high one.

There wasn't a car, a single person to be seen. Had she imagined it all? The unpleasant lads, going with Will to the cottage? Joel . . .? Linzi? Remembrance of Linzi's furious onslaught had Ella hurrying to the cottage, Oliver racing ahead.

Shutting the door behind them, Ella looked at the key in her hand. She knew she was being silly, but thrusting the key into the lock, she turned it. It was Oliver sitting hopefully by his food cupboard which made her realise she too was hungry. Feeding the dog first, she quickly made cheese sandwiches and then pouring a glass of apple juice, went up to her bedroom, to the window seat.

The exceptionally high tide now backed by a strong wind, Ella watched as waves came across the last few feet of sand, then over the shingle. Would her car be safe? But Audrey had said something about very high tides never reaching the cottage or the parking place, for they were on higher ground. She wasn't worried about her safety. The cottage had withstood far worse conditions than a frisky high tide.

The tide had turned, the setting sun glinting on the water, when Ellie remembered Oliver. Whatever else she thought about Will, he was fond of Oliver, would be worrying about him. So guessing Watch Cottage would be the first place he would come looking for his dog, she decided to take him home. But only as far as the little gate.

She was putting on her boots when someone passed the window, momentarily blocking out the light.

'Ella, are you there?'

It was Will!

Bending down, she held Oliver's muzzle to stop him barking. If she pressed herself against the wall, she might not be seen . . .

'Ella, I know you're there. Please let me in. let me explain. I know how it must have looked. If I could have left Linzi, I would have come after you. I've been so worried about you, but the tide . . .'

'If you were that worried, you could have waded through the water,' she called back.

Silence.

'There are phones!' she shouted.

'Just open the door! We can't sort things out like this.'

Ella did open it, but just enough to let Oliver out before slamming it shut again. Leaning against it, she held her breath. All she heard was the receding scrunch of Will's feet on the shingle, his low whistle to Oliver to follow.

*   *   *

It was dark when Ella made a sudden decision. She'd had enough. She didn't want to be with

115

people who enjoyed manipulating one another. Life was real, not some torturous game. The lives of Joel, Linzi and Will were tangled up together. She had to escape before she too became totally enmeshed.

'Sal, I'm leaving.' Standing by her loaded car, Ella was using her mobile phone. 'But I don't know what to do about the cottage.'

'What do you mean "leaving"?' Sal demanded so loudly that Ella smiled. She really didn't need the phone.

'I've . . . I've decided to go back to Worcester.'

'Why?'

'It hasn't worked out here.'

'What is this "it"?'

'I can't explain . . .'

'Then in that case, you'd better bring me the cottage keys.'

When Sal cut her off without another word, Ella stood looking at the silent phone. She had obviously upset the one person who had always shown her kindness.

Ella didn't look back as she drove up the hill. She had tried to conjure dreams about a new life but had failed. Reaching the top of the cliff, she pressed down on the accelerator so The Studio gate was only a blur in her headlights. She didn't slacken her speed, dare not in case Watch Cottage's magic drew her back.

Turning into Peace Farm yard, she suddenly

116

realised the enormity of what she was doing. She was letting Audrey down. Audrey had trusted her to look after her beloved Watch Cottage and now . . .

'Ella, come in before I catch a cold!'

Sal was standing in the open doorway, the light behind her showing she was in a dressing gown.

Picking up the cottage keys from the seat beside her, Ella opened the car door, then paused. What was she thinking of, disturbing Sal at night? She could have waited until morning. No she couldn't! Linzi, Joel and Will might . . .

'For goodness' sake, Ella . . . !'

Turning, Sal went back into the house, leaving the door open. Ella had planned on just handing over the keys and leaving quickly. Now she had no option.

'Sal?' she called, going towards the fire-lit kitchen.

'Sal?' Narrowing her eyes, she tried to distinguish what was substantial amongst the dancing shadows.

Then someone rose from a fireside chair.

'Will?'

'Sorry, you'll have to put up with me!'

It was Joel! She turned but he had moved swiftly to block her way, snapping on the light, dazzling her with its brightness.

'What are you doing here?' she demanded.

'I must talk to you.'

'I don't want to know! I saw you with Linzi at that church.'

'Which one of us were you spying on?' he drawled.

'I couldn't care less about you or Linzi.'

'Then why the half-implied accusation?'

'You were talking about Will as though . . . as though . . .'

'He didn't matter,' Joel finished. Then, 'Please Ella, don't go. Listen to me.'

When she shrugged, but didn't leave. Joel spoke slowly and so seriously that Ella realised this was a side of him she didn't know existed.

'As I expect you've guessed, Linzi is highly strung, at times irrational. Sometimes she thinks she's in love with me, sometimes it's Will.'

'But Will . . .'

'Doesn't love her. He's concerned about her, and sometimes he's the only one who can calm her.'

Ella closed her eyes as she saw again Will holding Linzi, talking softly to her.

'I know what happened,' Joel said. 'Will and I have talked.'

'You and Will?' she said incredulously.

'You see we had a common concern. You! But Linzi . . .'

'Oh I'm tired of hearing her name. Look, Will was far too concerned about her to bother about me, until he remembered Oliver and came for him.'

'That's not true. He didn't succeed in calming Linzi at Green Cottage. She got into her car and drove away like a maniac. He ran after her, I was driving along the road, saw him and stopped. When he told me what had happened, we decided we'd better find her before she did something silly.'

'What do you mean, "something silly"?'

'Crash the car, disappear for days. She often does that. So now do you see why Will worries about her, we both do.'

'Yes,' Ella said slowly. 'But I still think I should leave here.'

'Don't!' Sal had been standing on the darkened stairs listening. 'Don't ruin your life like I've done.' Coming to stand by Joel, she continued, 'You don't get many chances of finding happiness. I was selfish, threw mine away because I wouldn't take the time to understand my husband's side of things.'

'You think I should try to understand Linzi?' Ella asked incredulously.

It was Joel who replied with, 'No Ella, not Linzi . . . Will. Try to understand how he feels about Linzi, the position he's in. You wouldn't have him treat her unkindly, would you?'

'I guess not.'

Then she sighed with such a deep sadness, that Sal urged, 'Go to Will . . .'

'Go to Will? He left the cottage . . .'

'Because you wouldn't let him in!' Sal reminded sharply.

'How do you know that?'

'After Will left you, he phoned,' Sal said. 'He asked my advice. And it wasn't about Linzi! It was about you.'

'You all seem to have been very busy discussing me,' Ella said stiffly.

'That's because we all care about you in our different ways,' Joel replied. Then laughed, 'Don't look so scared! I'm not going to declare my undying love for you. Will and I found Linzi at a friend's house. As soon as he knew she was safe, Will left. Ella, it's hard for me to admit this, but I've played on her affection for Will to get at him. Then you came along, another one for me to use against him. Ella, Linzi doesn't really love him.'

'How can you be so sure?' she asked.

'I've persuaded her to forget Will. Not come back here again. I've been asked to do some photography near where she lives, so I'll be able to keep an eye on her. So that leaves Will free.'

'But suppose . . .' But even as she began voicing her doubts, relief flooded through Ella. If she and Will could have a fresh start . . .

'Go to him, Ella,' Sal said softly.

Both Sal and Joel nodded with satisfaction as they watched Ella turn left out of the farm. She was heading back to the bay. But would she stop at The Studio?

She didn't. She had a lot to think about before she saw Will. Nearing the end of the

120

road at the bay, the car headlights caught a dark shape by Watch Cottage. She stopped, her heart hammering. Had one of the noisy lads returned?

'Ella! It's me. Will!'

There was no mistaking his voice, the four-legged shape running towards her, barking.

It was then she realised there was no need to think about anything except turning off the car engine.

As she and Will ran towards each other Oliver frolicked about them. But when they kissed again and again, he flopped down on the turf and fell asleep.

'Look at Oliver,' Ella said, drawing away slightly in the circle of Will's arms. 'He's whimpering. He must be dreaming.'

'I think I must be too,' Will said. 'Ella darling, please stay. There's so much I want to share with you.'

'Like doing up holiday cottages?' she teased.

For a moment he looked at her blankly, then smiled. 'There's more to life than work. Much more. This for instance.'

His kisses left her in no doubt that the cottages were not what he had in mind!

Suddenly she tried to pull away. 'But how do you know?' she worried.

'Know what? That I love you? I used to think falling in love at first sight was romantic nonsense. But now I know it's not. Ella sweetheart, although we got off on the wrong foot, as soon as I saw you I knew deep down . . .'

'And so did I,' she whispered in wonder. 'But I thought it was impossible that you . . . It's magic, that's what it is! Magic,' she repeated dreamily. Then, 'I know, let's call your cottages Magic Touch. Holidaymakers' dreams of a perfect holiday.'

'And we, my own darling,' he said, glancing from her mouth to her eyes. 'Are already conjuring our own dreams.'